Frances Hodgson Burnett

was born in Manchester, England, on November 24, 1849. After her father's death in 1853, Burnett's mother ran the family's iron foundry until the American Civil War caused the business to fail. Destitute, the Hodgsons moved to Tennessee in 1865, to stay with relatives in a log cabin. Frances lived there until 1873, when she married a doctor, Swan Burnett, whom she later divorced in 1898. She married Peter Townesend, an actor, in 1900.

From her teens Frances had written stories and tales to help support the family and later claimed never to have written a manuscript that was not published. Her first widespread success came with *That Lass o' Lowrie's* in 1877, a tale of the Lancashire coal mines. But it was the publication of *Little Lord Fauntleroy*, in 1886, that brought the author fame and wealth and established Cedric as the model for a generation of young boys. *Sara Crewe* was published in 1888, and the rags-to-riches story was so successful that Burnett revised, expanded, and republished it in 1905 as *A Little Princess*. The beloved *The Secret Garden* appeared four years later to enormous critical and popular acclaim.

A prolific writer, Frances Hodgson Burnett wrote over 40 novels and plays and dozens of short stories during her lifetime. She died at Plandome, New York, on October 29, 1924.

Ask your bookseller for these other British Classics

BEOWULF AND OTHER OLD ENGLISH POEMS
    Translated by Constance B. Hieatt
THE CANTERBURY TALES by Geoffrey Chaucer
ROBINSON CRUSOE by Daniel Defoe
GULLIVER'S TRAVELS AND OTHER WRITINGS by Jonathan Swift
PRIDE AND PREJUDICE by Jane Austen
EMMA by Jane Austen
SENSE AND SENSIBILITY by Jane Austen
MANSFIELD PARK by Jane Austen
PERSUASION by Jane Austen
NORTHANGER ABBEY by Jane Austen
FRANKENSTEIN by Mary Shelley
JANE EYRE by Charlotte Brontë
VILLETTE by Charlotte Brontë
WUTHERING HEIGHTS by Emily Brontë
DAVID COPPERFIELD by Charles Dickens
GREAT EXPECTATIONS by Charles Dickens
HARD TIMES by Charles Dickens
OLIVER TWIST by Charles Dickens
A TALE OF TWO CITIES by Charles Dickens
NICHOLAS NICKLEBY by Charles Dickens
BLEAK HOUSE by Charles Dickens
THE PICKWICK PAPERS by Charles Dickens
A CHRISTMAS CAROL by Charles Dickens
A CHRISTMAS CAROL AND OTHER VICTORIAN FAIRY TALES by
    Charles Dickens
SILAS MARNER by George Eliot
MIDDLEMARCH by George Eliot
FAR FROM THE MADDING CROWD by Thomas Hardy
TESS OF THE D'URBERVILLES by Thomas Hardy
JUDE THE OBSCURE by Thomas Hardy
THE MAYOR OF CASTERBRIDGE by Thomas Hardy
THE RETURN OF THE NATIVE by Thomas Hardy
HEART OF DARKNESS and THE SECRET SHARER by Joseph Conrad
LORD JIM by Joseph Conrad
THE SECRET AGENT by Joseph Conrad
DR. JEKYLL AND MR. HYDE by Robert Louis Stevenson
TREASURE ISLAND by Robert Louis Stevenson
KIDNAPPED by Robert Louis Stevenson
DRACULA by Bram Stoker
CAPTAINS COURAGEOUS by Rudyard Kipling
KIM by Rudyard Kipling
THE JUNGLE BOOKS and JUST SO STORIES by Rudyard Kipling
THE SECRET GARDEN by Frances Hodgson Burnett
A LITTLE PRINCESS by Frances Hodgson Burnett
ALICE'S ADVENTURES IN WONDERLAND and THROUGH THE
    LOOKING-GLASS by Lewis Carroll
THE MOONSTONE by Wilkie Collins
THE WOMAN IN WHITE by Wilkie Collins
THE PICTURE OF DORIAN GRAY AND OTHER WRITINGS by Oscar Wilde
THE TIME MACHINE by H. G. Wells
THE INVISIBLE MAN by H. G. Wells
THE WIND IN THE WILLOWS by Kenneth Grahame
PETER PAN by J. M. Barrie
HOWARD'S END by E. M. Forster
LADY CHATTERLEY'S LOVER by D. H. Lawrence
SONS AND LOVERS by D. H. Lawrence

Little Lord Fauntleroy

by Frances Hodgson Burnett

With an Introduction
by Richard Peck

BANTAM BOOKS

TORONTO · NEW YORK · LONDON · SYDNEY · AUCKLAND

LITTLE LORD FAUNTLEROY
A Bantam Book

PRINTING HISTORY
First published in 1886
Bantam Classic edition / February 1987

Cover painting, Portrait of James Ward by Gilbert Stuart,
The Minneapolis Institute of Art.

ISBN 0-553-21202-8

Published simultaneously in the United States and Canada

PRINTED IN THE UNITED STATES OF AMERICA

O   0 9 8 7 6 5 4 3 2 1

CONTENTS

Introduction

Little Lord Fauntleroy, hero of a one hundred-year-old best-seller, is one of that handful of fictional characters whose names have entered the language. Never was a character from a novel more famous among people who never read the book.

His story is rudimentary and readable even when it twists. The overlooked heir of a British title is being reared obscurely in New York by his widowed American mother. His grandfather in the family castle sends for him, intending to transform him into a traditional young lordling. The tables turn. Small Cedric, Lord Fauntleroy, turns them. His old scoundrel of a grandfather is no match for Cedric's youthful, and American, innocence. The child converts the man. The author makes her theme crystal clear: "Nothing in the world is so strong as a kind heart." (p. 83) It was a recurring theme for Frances Hodgson Burnett: youthful American innocence blowing liberating breezes through older worlds.

And while the book's manners are picturesquely dated now, its theme is still a crowd pleaser. No one, not even the British nobility, has outlived the taste for a happy ending.

But no one in or out of literature ever suffered a worse reputation than Cedric Errol. For a stalwart American boy who not only does good, but does well, he's had an exceedingly bad rap. Even the name *Cedric* hasn't weathered the years well. He's the victim of his own author and an era when a small child was praised for acting like a grown-up. Worse, in the 1880s children were dressed to mimic famous paintings of bygone days. The most popular book illustrator of the time, Reginald Birch, condemns Cedric on the cover. Cedric's pictured as a creature of no particular sex with a yellow pageboy haircut and a black velvet suit with points of lace. He's hugging a dog.

Following the then current fashion, his author, Mrs. Burnett, makes matters worse. Cedric isn't even allowed to be a nice, basic, bald-headed baby. "He started in life with a quantity of soft, fine, gold-coloured hair, which curled up at the ends, and went into loose rings by the time he was six months old." (pp. 4–5) Never mind his strong back, his sturdy legs, and his ability to walk at nine months. No, his nurse dresses him in "a short white kilt skirt, and a big white hat set back on his curly yellow hair." (p. 5) Then when he can be freed of the dresses of infancy, his first black suit has to be made out of the velvet skirt of his mother's gown. His golden ringlets are by now described as "love-locks."

Even when Cedric is described as "one of the handsomest little fellows" (p. 21) ever seen, the author cannot restrain herself and speaks at once of his beauty.

These touches didn't damage his reputation when the book was new. The story was serialized in *St. Nicholas* magazine in 1885 and appeared as a book in 1886. As with its exact contemporary, *Huckleberry Finn*, its readership expanded quickly beyond children to include adults. But this considerable fame led to fresh difficulties for Cedric's image.

As early as 1888 the hit play based on the book starred a grown woman, the actress Elsie Leslie, in the role of seven-year-old Cedric Errol. It played for years. Like Peter Pan, he was destined to be impersonated by women, often. In 1921 Mary Pickford, "America's Sweetheart," portrayed him in a silent movie. Only in a 1936 film was this boy allowed to be played by a boy, Freddie Bartholomew. By then the damage was done, and the taste for velvet suits and lovelocks was decently buried under a mound of bib overalls and sneakers. And so Cedric Errol, Little Lord Fauntleroy, is due for an unbiased revival.

Cedric marches famously in a whole battalion of boys. Nineteenth-century literature kept discovering them and sending them out to pit their innocence against a jaded world. Cedric's challenge is an ancestral castle where broods an old reprobate grandfather with one leg propped on a gout stool.

Toby Tyler's great world is the harsh, spangled circus. Oliver Twist must rise from terrible depths, and Pip must realize his great expectations. Tom Brown's world to conquer is Rugby school, and Jim Hawkins's is Treasure Island.

"A good many distinguished men have once been poor boys," wrote the author of *Ragged Dick*, who should know because he was Horatio Alger, and he fathered more than his share.

Marching nearest Fauntleroy may well be the boys of Mark Twain. Huckleberry Finn, too, must set sail, literally, into a world of elders and old injustice. Marching closer still are Edward Tudor and Tom Canty, Twain's prince and pauper, who must try on each other's identity and fate.

The differences may lie more with the authors than with the boys. Only one of them was created by Frances Hodgson Burnett. Huckleberry's response to the Widow Douglas's precepts is light-years away from anything expressed by Cedric, who calls his widowed mother "Dearest" in imitation of his late father.

Tom Brown can't take his mother off to boarding school, and most of the other boys don't even have mothers. But when Cedric is sent for by the grandfather who hates his mother, she's allowed to go with him, against all odds. While Tom Sawyer's Aunt Polly " 'ain't got the heart to lash him somehow,' " Mrs. Errol would no more dream of whipping Cedric than of saying "ain't."

In a strong hint to her fellow parents, Mrs. Burnett points out that in childhood Cedric "had never heard an unkind or uncourteous word spoken at home." (p. 5)

The saintly Mrs. Errol, beautiful, modest, long-suffering, ultimately a winner, is the author's glossy self-portrait. When this perfect mother learns that her father-in-law and worst enemy is about to claim her only son, she says, " 'It will be best for my little boy. I know—I am sure the Earl would not be so unkind as to try to teach him not to love me; and I know—even if he tried—that my little boy is too much like his father to be harmed.' " (p. 19)

We're headed for trouble right there, as we come to the heart of the matter. The wicked old earl will do his dastardly best to destroy this mother-son relationship. " 'Give him what will amuse him, and he'll forget about his mother quickly enough.' " (p. 77)

But nothing works the earl's way. He buys Cedric toys and is himself lured into innocent boyhood, when Cedric teaches him to play. He buys the boy a pony, and Cedric only wants to go to his mother to tell her of Grandfather's generosity. Never having heard of a father who loathes his own sons, Cedric assumes that the old man is mourning their deaths. Acting for him, Cedric, at seven, begins to improve the lives of the estate tenants.

Generations of critics have skewered Cedric as a little do-gooding milksop, or worse. But they miss the point. Never having encountered evil, Cedric attributes to Grandfather uniformly good motives. The irony works, and the old beast is redeemed. Watching him led by a child into a life worth living remains the pleasure it was meant to be. Fortunately, the old earl is redeemable, and witty enough to observe his own conversion. "To see each of his ugly, selfish motives changed into a good and generous one by the simplicity of a child was a singular experience." (p. 89)

The old gent is redeemed as much by his own sense of irony. To a terrified tenant he remarks, " 'You people have been mistaken in me. Lord Fauntleroy understands me. When you want reliable information on the subject of my charter, apply to him. Get into the carriage, Fauntleroy.' '' (p. 100) This is good stuff. The tenants understand him only too well; it's his grandson alone who merely believes him good and thus makes him so.

When the earl provides his dreaded daughter-in-law with ''a pretty little brougham and a handsome bay horse,'' so she need not walk to perform her own good works, we know he's about to be transformed ''into quite a well-behaved old nobleman.'' (p. 169)

Little Lord Fauntleroy also deals with that perennially popular subject, the class system. Following the goings-on in the British system remains one of America's most popular entertainments, whether the royal weddings of princes in the 1980s or a small boy plucked from American exile and turned into a lord in the 1880s.

The English hierarchy is thus given quite a satisfactory airing in this book, both upstairs and downstairs. At the very head of the stairs is Cedric's grandfather, John Arthur Molyneux Errol, with four hundred years of tyrannical titledom behind him. He's a curmudgeon with broad hints of the corrupt. We can shake our American heads at the luxurious idleness of his long life, for he's used his ''strength and wealth and power only to please himself and kill time.'' (p. 91)

He isn't called the ''wicked Earl of Dorincourt'' for nothing. He despises everyone beneath him and recognizes nobody above. He hates all Americans, particularly Cedric's flawless mother. And he has a special antipathy for the young. '' 'Children are usually idiots or bores—mine were both.' '' (p. 127)

This egregious earl is attended by those other stock favorites: a cast of perfect servants unobtainable elsewhere at any price. They mirror their master's world. In fact, they can outdo him:

The big footman almost perilled his reputation
and his situation by smiling. He was an aristocratic
footman who had always lived in the best of noble
families, and he had never smiled, indeed he would
have felt himself a disgraced and vulgar footman if
he had allowed himself to be led by any circumstances whatever into such an indiscretion as a
smile. But he had a very narrow escape. He only
just saved himself by staring straight over the Earl's
head at a very ugly picture. (p. 64)

The earl, in short, is a sort of landed and titled Ebenezer
Scrooge, except he's no miser. His author was herself too
fond of lavish sets and grand gestures, manicured gardens and
good furniture. The earl lives baronially at Dorincourt Castle,
while at the other end of the long drive is a dower house
suitable for keeping a despised daughter-in-law in her place.
Beyond lies the necessary English village with a gossipy
church and a hard-pressed clergyman. The damp village cottages
are full of the deserving poor, who've been waiting centuries
for a lord of the manor to improve their lot. Help is here.
Though off our turf, we're on familiar ground.

But Frances Hodgson Burnett creates, perhaps uninten-
tionally, a sharper view of the American class system, and
it's more interesting to us than to her first readers. We see
that a century ago the Irish in New York were an underclass
suitable only for character parts. They speak a brogue that
was thought side-splittingly funny at the time. Moreover,
Cedric and his mother are Republicans in a sea of Irish
Democrats. Here is Mary, the servant, on the subject of
Cedric, who at the age of seven is already reading the
newspaper:

" 'Mary,' sez he, 'I'm very much int'rusted in
the 'lection,' sez he. 'I'm a 'publican, an' so is
Dearest. Are you a 'publican, Mary?' 'Sorra a bit,'
sez I; 'I'm the bist o' Dimmycrats!' An' he looks up

at me wid a look that ud go to yer heart, an' sez he:
'Mary,' sez he, 'the country will go to ruin.' An'
nivver a day since thin has he let go by widout
argyin' wid me to change me polytics.' '' (p. 6-7)

Midway between the Irish immigrants and Cedric's gen-
teelly impoverished mother is Mr. Hobbs, the grocer, embody-
ing the solid merchant class. Hobbs, who discusses politics
and primogeniture with Cedric among the biscuit barrels of
his corner store, is the novel's most entertaining character.

New Yorkers then as now were not well acquainted with
life beyond their city limits. But Mr. Hobbs is a staunchly
American Anglophobe who reads the *Illustrated London News*.
A flag-waving Yankee patriot, he inveighs against the injus-
tices of England.

"Being specially indignant against earls and marquises,"
(p. 8) he's struck not quite speechless when Cedric turns out
to be gentry. This is our opportunity to watch Hobbs reverse
himself and revise his views, though not before he mixes up
his monarchs. He confuses the present Queen Victoria with
the historic Bloody Mary and fears for the heads of all
involved. " 'Just let a woman like that get mad, an' no one's
safe!' '' (p. 141) And then the final shocker. It dawns on him
that the British don't celebrate the Fourth of July.

When things take "an uniggspected turn," Mr. Hobbs
ends up in England, a convert of course, but even there he's
shown a gallery of family portraits only to confuse *ancestors*
with *aunt-sisters*. He's played for all he's worth, and he's
very good value.

He ends up as a British shopkeeper catering to the
aristocracy. From there he can engage in that most American
of pastimes: criticizing America. " 'It's a good enough country for them that's young an' stirrin'—but there's faults in it.
There's not an aunt-sister among 'em—nor a earl!' '' (p.
172)

Hobbs has the final word in the novel, but there's some

last-minute nonsense about a young rival to Little Lord Fauntleroy's title, with a scar on his chin that disproves his claim. But we're neither troubled nor deceived. This isn't one more cliff-hanger in a century full of them. Cedric is never seriously threatened with defeat. This isn't a tale about the struggle for power and position. This is a story about the superior strength of innocence over experience, of goodness over error. It foreshadows a good many twentieth-century television shows and films about the superior wisdom of children, including every movie Shirley Temple ever made.

And lest we get too carried away with Old World grandeur and intrigue, we have earthy Mr. Hobbs to keep us steady. " 'It was a pity to make an earl out of him. He would have *shone* in the grocery business—or dry goods either; he would have *shone*!' " (p. 138)

Little Lord Fauntleroy would have shone anywhere, but is he hopelessly out of date? No. His is a story about the permissively reared child of a single parent, a child who rises in life beyond all parental expectation and isn't spoiled by it. We'll always need such hopeful stories, and never more than now.

Could Fauntleroy actually have existed? Maybe not, but it's pleasant to think he might have gone on living in whatever parallel world famous fictional characters inhabit.

Would he have inherited the title to become the earl of Dorincourt? Certainly, and soon, for the old earl is on his last legs. Would Cedric's mother have spared him to school? Yes, because she's the perfect mother. He'd have gone off to Eton, a family tradition, to be an athlete there. His grandfather introduced him to the mysteries of cricket, and he's already a sturdy-legged runner. He'd have brought his friends home to the castle for holidays because an earl has many friends, and this one is generous to a fault.

He'd certainly have gone on to Oxbridge University. After all, he's academically gifted. He's reading and writing miles above grade level at age seven, though his spelling is shaky.

He'd have been a soldier, in the full understanding that Britain and America never fight each other. His father was a soldier, and he admires General Washington. He'd have been a young officer in the Boer War and a more seasoned one in World War I.

By then he'd have married one of the much younger sisters of the Miss Herbert who wafts so beguilingly through his book. Doubtless there'd be another heir, a twentieth-century Lord Fauntleroy, who might be a little harder to handle than his father had been.

Cedric would have aged more gracefully than his reputation through changing times. The horses in his stable would have given way to Rolls-Royces, to grow old in their own time. The staff of servants would have dwindled inevitably. He might have ended a long and public-spirited life by opening Dorincourt Castle to American tourists. Let's leave him greeting them in well-weathered tweeds, free at last of the black velvet suit made from the skirt of his late mother's gown.

There's another story, which Frances Hodgson Burnett never wrote, though it has all the elements to appeal to her and her vast public.

It's the farfetched tale of a Victorian English girl whose merchant father dies young, leaving a widow to the struggle of providing for four children. The family finally faces starvation when effects of the Civil War in America ruin the cotton-spinning economy of Manchester, England. The widow contrives to take her children on a tempest-tossed voyage to the United States, where their Uncle William is a shopkeeper in the Tennessee Mountains. His niece improves her storytelling skills before an audience of her siblings seated around the fireplace of a log cabin. Soon she's gathering wild grapes to sell for postage money to send her stories off to *Godey's Lady's Book*.

Rags-to-riches again?

Yes. From the first, she's a best-selling author in both her countries. Her creations are stories and plays of childhood optimism and adult intrigue, always glamorously adorned, in which the wished-for becomes real.

She marries an eminent doctor and has sons that she dresses like small English gentlemen, even in that political outpost, Washington, D.C. They live in a series of increasingly fine houses surrounded by splendid gardens in Italy, Bermuda, America, England. Our heroine grows grander than a duchess and moves in the court society of the country where she once nearly starved to death. She endures the death of a son in childhood. She glories in the love of another son, whose biography of her is entitled *Dearest*.

Like most of the mighty, she is touched with scandal. This living symbol of Victorian propriety divorces her husband and stuns her friends by marrying a much younger man, an actor in a dramatization of her most famous work.

She lives a long life, a friend of the famous in many worlds, from President Garfield to Henry James. To the end she remains a favorite of readers who share all her hopes for happily-ever-after. She dies in a vast canopied bed in an English country house set in a Long Island garden, facing a long window looking out on the sunset.

That was Frances Eliza Hodgson Burnett's life as she lived it. Known in her own time for her work for adult readers and playgoers, she's remembered for her special worlds of childhood: *The Secret Garden, Little Saint Elizabeth, Sara Crewe*, which she expanded and republished as *A Little Princess*. But in her own life she was the doting mother of sons, and she captured them both to create her most lasting character, Cedric Errol, Little Lord Fauntleroy.

RICHARD PECK

Little Lord Fauntleroy

ONE

A Great Surprise

Cedric himself knew nothing whatever about it. It had never been even mentioned to him. He knew that his papa had been an Englishman, because his mamma had told him so; but then his papa had died when he was so little a boy that he could not remember very much about him, except that he was big, and had blue eyes and a long moustache, and that it was a splendid thing to be carried around the room on his shoulder. Since his papa's death, Cedric had found out that it was best not to talk to his mamma about him. When his father was ill, Cedric had been sent away, and when he had returned, everything was over; and his mother, who had been very ill too, was only just beginning to sit in her chair by the window. She was pale and thin, and all the dimples had gone from her pretty face and her eyes looked large and mournful, and she was dressed in black.

'Dearest,' said Cedric (his papa had called her that always, and so the little boy had learned to say it), 'Dearest, is my papa better?'

He felt her arms tremble, and so he turned his curly head, and looked in her face. There was something in it that made him feel that she was going to cry.

'Dearest,' he said, 'is he well?'

Then suddenly his loving little heart told him that he'd better put both his arms around her neck and kiss her again and again, and keep his soft cheek close to hers; and he did so, and she laid her face on his shoulder and cried bitterly, holding him as if she could never let him go again.

'Yes, he is well,' she sobbed; 'he is quite, quite well, but we—we have no one left but each other. No one at all.'

Then, little as he was, he understood that his big, handsome young papa would not come back any more; that he was dead, as he had heard of other people being, although he could not comprehend exactly what strange thing had brought all this sadness about. It was because his mamma always cried when he spoke of his papa that he secretly made up his mind it was better not to speak of him very often to her, and he found out, too, that it was better not to let her sit still and look into the fire or out of the window without moving or talking. He and his mamma knew very few people, and lived what might have been thought very lonely lives, although Cedric did not know it was lonely until he grew older and heard why it was they had no visitors. Then he was told that his mamma was an orphan, and quite alone in the world when his papa had married her. She was very pretty, and had been living as companion to a rich old lady who was not kind to her, and one day Captain Cedric Errol, who was calling at the house, saw her run up the stairs with tears on her eyelashes; and she looked so sweet and innocent and sorrowful that the Captain could not forget her. And after many strange things had happened, they knew each other well and loved each other dearly, and were married, although their marriage brought them the ill-will of several persons. The one who was most angry of all, however, was the Captain's father, who lived in England, and was a very rich and important old nobleman, with a very bad temper, and a very violent dislike to America and Americans. He had two sons older than Captain Cedric; and it was the law that the elder of these sons should inherit the family title and estates, which were very rich and splendid; if the eldest son died the next one would be heir; so though he was a member of such a great family, there was little chance that Captain Cedric would be very rich himself.

But it so happened that Nature had given to the younger son gifts which she had not bestowed upon his elder brothers. He had a beautiful face and a fine, strong, graceful figure; he had a bright smile and a sweet, gay voice; he was brave and generous, and had the kindest heart in the world, and seemed to have the power to make everyone love him. But it was not so with his elder brothers; neither of them was handsome, or very kind or clever. When they were boys at Eton, they were not popular; when they were at college, they cared nothing for study, and wasted both time and money, and made few real friends. The old Earl, their father, was constantly disappointed and humiliated by them; his heir was no honour to his noble name, and did not promise to end in being anything but a selfish, wasteful, insignificant man, with no manly or noble qualities. It was very bitter, the old Earl thought, that the son who was only third, and would have only a very small fortune, should be the one who had all the gifts, and all the charms, and all the strength and beauty. Sometimes he almost hated the handsome young man because he seemed to have the good things which should have gone with the stately title and the magnificent estates; and yet, in the depths of his proud, stubborn old heart, he could not help caring very much for his youngest son. It was in one of his fits of petulance that he sent him off to travel in America; he thought he would send him away for a while, so that he should not be made angry by constantly contrasting him with his brothers, who were at that time giving him a great deal of trouble by their wild ways.

But after about six months, he began to feel lonely, and longed in secret to see his son again, so he wrote to Captain Cedric and ordered him home. The letter he wrote crossed on its way a letter the Captain had just written to his father telling of his love for the pretty American girl, and of his intended marriage; and when the Earl received that letter, he was furiously angry. Bad as his temper was, he had never given way to it in his life as he gave way to it when he read the Captain's letter. His valet, who was in the room when it came, thought his lordship would have a fit of apoplexy, he was so wild with anger. For an hour he raged like a tiger, and then he sat down and wrote to his son, and ordered him never to come near his old home, nor to write to his father or brothers again. He told him he might live as he pleased, and die where he pleased, that he should be cut off from his family for ever, and that he need never expect help from his father as long as he lived.

The Captain was very sad when he read the letter; he was very fond of England, and he dearly loved the beautiful home where he had been born; he had even loved his ill-tempered old father, and had sympathized with him in his disappointments; but he knew he need expect no kindness from him in the future. At first he scarcely knew what to do; he had not been brought up to work, and had no business experience, but he had courage and plenty of determination. So he sold his commission in the English army, and after some trouble found a situation in New York, and married. The change from his old life in England was very great, but he was young and happy and he hoped that hard work would do great things for him in the future. He had a small house in a quiet street, and his little boy was born there, and everything was so gay and cheerful, in a simple way, that he was never sorry for a moment that he had married the rich old lady's pretty companion just because she was so sweet and he loved her and she loved him. She was very sweet indeed, and her little boy was like both her and his father. Though he was born in so quiet and cheap a little home, it seemed as if there never had been a more fortunate baby. In the first place he was always well, and so he never gave anyone trouble; in the second place he had so sweet a temper and ways so charming that he was a pleasure to everyone; and in the third place he was so beautiful to look at that he was quite a picture. Instead of being a bald-headed baby, he started in life with a quantity of soft, fine, gold-coloured hair, which curled up at the ends, and went into loose rings by the time he was six months old; he had big brown eyes and long eyelashes and a darling little face; he had so strong a back and splendid sturdy legs that at nine months he learned suddenly to walk; his manners were so good, for a baby, that it was delightful to make his acquaintance. He seemed to feel that everyone was his friend, and when anyone spoke to him, when he was in his carriage in the street, he would give the stranger one sweet serious look with the brown eyes, and then follow in with a lovely, friendly smile; and the consequence was, that there was not a person in the neighbourhood of the quiet street where he lived—even to the grocery-man at the corner, who was considered the crossest creature alive—who was not pleased to see him, and speak to him. And every month of his life he grew handsomer and more interesting.

When he was old enough to walk out with his nurse, dragging a small wagon and wearing a short white kilt skirt, and a big white hat set back on his curly yellow hair, he was so handsome and strong and rosy that he attracted everyone's attention, and his nurse would come home and tell his mamma stories of the ladies who had stopped their carriages to look at and speak to him, and of how pleased they were when he talked to them in his cheerful little way, as if he had known them always. His greatest charm was this cheerful, fearless, quaint little way of making friends with people. I think it arose from his having a very confiding nature, and a kind little heart that sympathized with everyone, and wished to make everyone as comfortable as he liked to be himself. It made him very quick to understand the feelings of those about him. Perhaps this had grown on him too, because he had lived so much with his father and mother, who were always loving and considerate and tender and well bred. He had never heard an unkind or uncourteous word spoken at home; he had always been loved and caressed and treated tenderly, and so his childish soul was full of kindness and innocent warm feeling. He had always heard his mamma called by pretty, loving names, and so he used them himself when he spoke to her; he had always seen that his papa watched over her and took great care of her, and so he learned too to be careful of her.

So when he knew his papa would come back no more and saw how very sad his mamma was, there gradually came into his kind little heart the thought that he must do what he could to make her happy. He was not much more than a baby, but that thought was in his mind whenever he climbed upon her knee and kissed her, and put his curly head on her neck, and when he brought his toys and picture books to show her, and when he curled up quietly by her side as she used to lie on the sofa. He was not old enough to know of anything else to do, so he did what he could, and was more of a comfort to her than he could have understood.

'Oh, Mary,' he heard her say once to her old servant, 'I am sure he is trying to help me in his innocent way—I know he is. He looks at me sometimes with a loving, wondering little look, as if he were sorry for me, and then he will come and pet me or show me something. He is such a little man, I really think he knows.'

As he grew older he had a great many quaint little ways which amused and interested people greatly. He was so much of a companion for his mother that she scarcely cared for any other. They used to walk together and talk together and play together. When he was quite a little fellow he learned to read; and after that he used to lie on the hearthrug, in the evening, and read aloud—sometimes stories, and sometimes big books such as older people read, and sometimes even the newspaper; and often at such times Mary, in the kitchen, would hear Mrs Errol laughing with delight at the quaint things he said.

'And, indade,' said Mary to the grocery-man, 'nobody cud help laughin' at the quare little ways of him—and his ould-fashioned sayin's! Didn't he come into my kitchen the noight the new prisident was nominated and shtand afore the fire, lookin' loike a pictur', wid his hands in his shmall pockets, an' his innocent bit of a face as sayrious as a jedge? An' sez he to me: "Mary," sez he, "I'm very much int'rusted in the 'lection," sez he. "I'm a 'publican, an' so is Dearest. Are you a 'publican, Mary?" "Sorra a bit," sez I; "I'm the bist o' dimmycrats!" An' he looks up at me wid a look that ud go to yer heart, an' sez he: "Mary," sez he, "the country will go to ruin." An' nivver a day since thin has he let go by widout argyin' wid me to change me polytics.'

Mary was very fond of him, and very proud of him too. She had been with his mother ever since he was born; and after his father's death, had been cook and housemaid and nurse and everything else. She was proud of his graceful, strong little body and his pretty manners, especially proud of the bright curly hair which waved over his forehead and fell in charming love-locks on his shoulders. She was willing to work early and late to help his mamma to make his small suits and keep them in order.

'Ristycratic, is it?' she would say. 'Faith and I'd loike to see the choild on Fifth Avey-*noo* as he looks loike him an' shteps out as handsome as himself. An' ivvery man, woman and choild lookin' afther him in his bit of a black velvet skirt made out of the misthress's ould gownd; an' his little head up an' his curly hair flyin' an' shinin'. It's like a young lord he looks.'

Cedric did not know that he looked like a young lord; he did not know what a lord was. His greatest friend was the grocery-man at the corner—the cross grocery-man, who was never cross to him. His name was Mr Hobbs, and Cedric admired and respected him very much. He thought him a very rich and powerful person, he had so many things in his store—prunes and figs and oranges and biscuits—and he had a horse and wagon. Cedric was fond of the milkman and the baker and the apple-woman, but he liked Mr Hobbs best of all, and was on terms of such intimacy with him that he went to see him every day, and often sat with him quite a long time discussing the topics of the hour. It was quite surprising how many things they found to talk about—the Fourth of July, for instance. When they began to talk about the Fourth of July there really seemed no end to it. Mr Hobbs had a very bad

opinion of 'the British', and he told the whole story of the
Revolution, relating very wonderful and patriotic stories about
the villainy of the enemy and the bravery of the revolutionary
heroes, and he even generously repeated part of the Declaration of Independence. Cedric was so excited that his eyes
shone and his cheeks were red and his curls were all rubbed
and tumbled into a yellow mop. He could hardly wait to eat
his dinner after he went home, he was so anxious to tell his
mamma. It was perhaps Mr Hobbs who gave him his first
interest in politics. Mr Hobbs was fond of reading the
newspapers, and so Cedric heard a great deal about what was
going on in Washington; and Mr Hobbs would tell him
whether the President was doing his duty or not. And once,
when there was an election, he found it all quite grand, and
probably but for Mr Hobbs and Cedric the country might
have been wrecked. Mr Hobbs took him to see a great
torchlight procession, and many of the men who carried
torches remembered afterwards a stout man who stood near a
lamppost and held on his shoulder a handsome little shouting
boy, who waved his cap in the air.

It was not long after this election, when Cedric was
between seven and eight years old, that the very strange thing
happened which made so wonderful a change in his life. It
was quite curious, too, that the day it happened he had been
talking to Mr Hobbs about England and the Queen, and Mr
Hobbs had said some very severe things about the aristocracy,
being specially indignant against earls and marquises. It had
been a hot morning, and after playing soldiers with some
friends of his, Cedric had gone into the store to rest, and had
found Mr Hobbs looking very fierce over a piece of the
Illustrated London News, which contained a picture of some
Court ceremony.

'Ah,' he said, 'that's the way they go on now; but
they'll get enough of it some day, when those they've trod on
rise and blow 'em up sky-high—earls and markises and all!
It's coming, and they may look out for it!'

Cedric had perched himself as usual on the high stool

and pushed his hat back, and put his hands in his pockets in delicate compliment to Mr Hobbs.

'Did you ever know many marquises, Mr Hobbs?' Cedric inquired; 'or earls?'

'No,' answered Mr Hobbs with indignation; 'I guess not. I'd like to catch one of 'em inside here; that's all! I'll have no grasping tyrants sittin' 'round on my biscuit barrels!'

And he was so proud of the sentiment that he looked around proudly and mopped his forehead.

'Perhaps they wouldn't be earls if they knew any better,' said Cedric, feeling some vague sympathy for their unhappy condition.

'Wouldn't they!' said Mr Hobbs. 'They just glory in it! It's in 'em. They're a bad lot.'

They were in the midst of their conversation when Mary appeared. Cedric thought she had come to buy some sugar, perhaps, but she had not. She looked almost pale as if she were excited about something.

'Come home, darlint,' she said; 'the misthress is wantin' yez.'

Cedric slipped down from his stool. 'Does she want me to go out with her, Mary?' he asked. 'Good morning, Mr Hobbs. I'll see you again.'

He was surprised to see Mary staring at him in a dumbfounded fashion, and he wondered why she kept shaking her head. 'What's the matter, Mary?' he said. 'Is it the hot weather?'

'No,' said Mary, 'but there's strange things happenin' to us.'

'Has the sun given Dearest a headache?' he inquired anxiously.

But it was not that. When he reached his own house there was a coupé standing before the door, and someone was in the little parlour talking to his mamma. Mary hurried him upstairs and put on his best summer suit of cream-coloured flannel with the red scarf around the waist, and combed out his curly locks.

'Lords, is it?' he heard her say. 'An' the nobility an' gintry. Och! bad cess to them! Lords indade—worse luck.'

It was really very puzzling, but he felt sure his mamma would tell him what all the excitement meant, so he allowed Mary to bemoan herself without asking many questions. When he was dressed, he ran downstairs and went into the parlour. A tall, thin old gentleman with a sharp face was sitting in an armchair. His mother was standing near by with a pale face, and he saw that there were tears in her eyes.

'Oh, Ceddie!' she cried out, and ran to her little boy and caught him in her arms and kissed him in a little frightened, troubled way. 'Oh, Ceddie darling!'

The tall old gentleman rose from his chair and looked at Cedric with his sharp eyes. He rubbed his thin chin with his bony hand as he looked. He seemed not at all displeased.

'And so,' he said at last slowly, 'and so this is little Lord Fauntleroy.'

TWO

Cedric's Friends

There was never a more amazed little boy than Cedric during the week that followed; there was never so strange or so unreal a week. In the first place, the story his mamma told him was a very curious one. He was obliged to hear it two or three times before he could understand it. He could not imagine what Mr Hobbs would think of it. It began with earls; his grandpapa, whom he had never seen, was an earl; and his eldest uncle, if he had not been killed by a fall from his horse, would have been an earl too in time; and after his death, his other uncle would have been an earl, if he had not died suddenly, in Rome, of fever. After that, his own papa, if he had lived, would have been an earl; but since they had all died and only Cedric was left, it appeared that *he* was to be an earl after his grandpapa's death—and for the present he was Lord Fauntleroy.

He turned quite pale when he was first told of it.

'Oh, Dearest,' he said, 'I should rather not be an earl. None of the boys are earls. Can't I *not* be one?'

But it seemed to be unavoidable. And when, that evening, they sat together by the open window looking out into the shabby street, he and his mother had a long talk about it. Cedric sat on his footstool, clasping one knee in his favourite

11

attitude and wearing a bewildered little face rather red from
the exertion of thinking. His grandfather had sent for him to
come to England and his mamma thought he must go.

'Because,' she said, looking out of the window with
sorrowful eyes, 'I know your papa would wish it to be so,
Ceddie. He loved his home very much; and there are many
things to be thought of that a little boy can't quite understand.
I should be a selfish little mother if I did not send you. When
you are a man you will see why.'

Ceddie shook his head mournfully. 'I shall be very sorry
to leave Mr Hobbs,' he said. 'I'm afraid he'll miss me, and I
shall miss him. And I shall miss them all.'

When Mr Havisham—who was the family lawyer of the
Earl of Dorincourt, and who had been sent by him to bring
Lord Fauntleroy to England—came the next day, Cedric heard
many things. But somehow it did not console him to hear that
he was to be a very rich man when he grew up, and that he
would have castles here and castles there, and great parks and
deep mines and grand estates and tenantry. He was troubled
about his friend, Mr Hobbs, and he went to see him at the
store soon after breakfast in great anxiety of mind.

He found him reading the morning paper, and he approached him with a grave demeanour. He really felt it would
be a great shock to Mr Hobbs to hear what had befallen him,
and on his way to the store he had been thinking how it
would be best to break the news.

'Hallo!' said Mr Hobbs. 'Mornin'!'

'Good morning,' said Cedric.

He did not climb up on the high stool as usual but sat
down on a biscuit box and clasped his knee, and was so silent
for a few moments that Mr Hobbs finally looked up inquir-
ingly over the top of his newspaper.

'Hallo!' he said again.

Cedric gathered all his strength of mind together.

'Mr Hobbs,' he said, 'do you remember what we were
talking about yesterday morning?'

'Well,' replied Mr Hobbs, 'seems to me it was England.'

'Yes,' said Cedric; 'but just when Mary came for me, you know?'

Mr Hobbs rubbed the back of his head.

'We *was* mentioning Queen Victoria and the aristocracy.'

'Yes,' said Cedric rather hesitantly, 'and—and earls; don't you know?'

'Why, yes,' returned Mr Hobbs; 'we *did* touch 'em up a little; that's so!'

Cedric flushed up to the curly hair on his forehead. Nothing so embarrassing as this had ever happened to him in his life. He was a little afraid that it might be a trifle embarrassing to Mr Hobbs too.

'You said,' he proceeded, 'that you wouldn't have them sitting 'round on your biscuit barrels.'

'So I did!' returned Mr Hobbs stoutly. 'And I meant it. Let 'em try it—that's all!'

'Mr Hobbs,' said Cedric, 'one is sitting on this box now!'

Mr Hobbs almost jumped out of his chair.

'What!' he exclaimed.

'Yes,' Cedric announced with due modesty; '*I* am one—or I am going to be. I shan't deceive you.'

Mr Hobbs looked agitated. He rose up suddenly and went to look at the thermometer.

'The mercury's got into your head!' he exclaimed, turning back to examine his young friend's countenance. 'It *is* a hot day! How do you feel? Got any pain? When did you begin to feel that way?'

He put his big hand on the little boy's hair. This was more embarrassing than ever.

'Thank you,' said Ceddie; 'I'm all right. There is nothing the matter with my head. I'm sorry to say it's true, Mr Hobbs. That was what Mary came to take me home for. Mr Havisham was telling my mamma, and he is a lawyer.'

Mr Hobbs sank into his chair and mopped his forehead with his handkerchief.

'*One* of us has got a sunstroke!' he exclaimed.

'No,' returned Cedric, 'we have not. We shall have to make the best of it, Mr Hobbs. Mr Havisham came all the way from England to tell us about it. My grandpapa sent him.'

Mr Hobbs stared wildly at the innocent, serious little face before him.

'Who is your grandfather?' he asked.

Cedric put his hand in his pocket and carefully drew out a piece of paper, on which something was written in his own round, irregular hand.

'I couldn't easily remember it, so I wrote it down on this,' he said. And he read aloud slowly: ' ''John Arthur Molyneux Errol, Earl of Dorincourt''. That is his name, and he lives in a castle—in two or three castles, I think. And my papa, who died, was his youngest son; and I shouldn't have been a lord or an earl if my papa hadn't died; and my papa wouldn't have been an earl if his two brothers hadn't died. But they all died, and there is no one but me—no boy—and so I have to be one; and my grandpapa has sent for me to come to England.'

Mr Hobbs seemed to grow hotter and hotter. He mopped his forehead and his bald spot and breathed hard. He began to see that something very remarkable had happened; but when he looked at the little boy sitting on the biscuit box with the innocent, anxious expression in his childish eyes, and saw that he was not changed at all, but was simply as he had been the day before, just a handsome, cheerful, brave little fellow in a black cloth suit and red neck-ribbon, all this information about the nobility bewildered him. He was all the more bewildered because Cedric gave it with such ingenuous simplicity and plainly without realizing himself how stupendous it was.

'Wha—what did you say your name was?' Mr Hobbs inquired.

'It's Cedric Errol, Lord Fauntleroy,' answered Cedric. 'That was what Mr Havisham called me. He said when I went into the room: ''And so this is little Lord Fauntleroy!'' '

'Well,' said Mr Hobbs, 'I'll be—jiggered!'

This was an exclamation he always used when he was very much astonished or excited. He could think of nothing else to say just at that puzzling moment.

Cedric felt it to be quite a proper and suitable ejaculation. His respect and affection for Mr Hobbs were so great that he admired and approved of all his remarks. He had not seen enough of society as yet to make him realize that sometimes Mr Hobbs was not quite conventional. He knew, of course, that he was different from his mamma, but then his mamma was a lady, and he had an idea that ladies were always different from gentlemen.

He looked at Mr Hobbs wistfully.

'England is a long way off, isn't it?' he asked.

'It's across the Atlantic Ocean,' Mr Hobbs answered.

'That's the worst of it,' said Cedric. 'Perhaps I shall not see you again for a long time. I don't like to think of that, Mr Hobbs.'

'The best of friends must part,' said Mr Hobbs.

'Well,' said Cedric, 'we have been friends for a great many years, haven't we?'

'Ever since you was born,' Mr Hobbs answered. 'You was about six weeks old when you were first walked out on this street.'

'Ah,' remarked Cedric with a sigh, 'I never thought I should have to be an earl then!'

'You think,' said Mr Hobbs, 'there's no getting out of it?'

'I'm afraid not,' answered Cedric. 'My mamma says that my papa would wish me to do it. But if I have to be an earl, there's one thing I can do: I can try to be a good one. I'm not going to be a tyrant. And if there is ever to be another war with America I shall try to stop it.'

His conversation with Mr Hobbs was a long and serious one. Once having got over the first shock, Mr Hobbs was not so rancourous as might have been expected; he endeavoured to resign himself to the situation, and before the interview was at an end he had asked a great many questions. As Cedric could answer but few of them he endeavoured to answer them himself, and being fairly launched on the subject of earls and marquises and lordly estates, explained many things in a way which would probably have astonished Mr Havisham, could that gentleman have heard it.

But then there were many things which astonished Mr Havisham. He had spent all his life in England, and was not accustomed to American people and American habits. He had been connected professionally with the family of the Earl of Dorincourt for nearly forty years, and he knew all about its grand estates and its great wealth and importance; and, in a cold business-like way, he felt an interest in this little boy who, in the future, was to be the master and owner of them all—the future Earl of Dorincourt. He had known all about the old Earl's disappointment in his elder sons and all about his fierce rage at Captain Cedric's American marriage, and he knew how he still hated the gentle little widow and would not speak of her except with bitter and cruel words. He insisted that she was only a common American girl who had entrapped his son into marrying her because she knew he was an earl's son. The old lawyer himself had more than half believed this was all true. He had seen a great many selfish, mercenary people in his life, and he had not a good opinion of Americans. When he had been driven into the cheap street, and his coupé had stopped before the cheap small house, he had felt actually shocked. It seemed really quite dreadful to think that the future owner of Dorincourt Castle and Wyndham Towers and Chorlworth, and all the other stately splendours, should have been born and brought up in an insignificant house in a street with a sort of green-grocery at the corner. He wondered what kind of a child he would be, and what kind of a mother he had. He rather shrank from seeing them both. He had a sort of pride in the noble family whose legal affairs he had conducted so long, and it would have annoyed him very much to have found himself obliged to manage a woman who would seem to him a vulgar, money-loving person, with no respect for her dead husband's country and the dignity of his name. It was a very old name and a very splendid one, and Mr Havisham had a great respect for it himself though he was only a cold, keen business-like old lawyer.

When Mary handed him into the small parlour he looked around it critically. It was plainly furnished, but it had a home-like look; there were no cheap, common ornaments, and no cheap, gaudy pictures; the few adornments on the walls were in good taste, and about the room were many pretty things which a woman's hand might have made.

'Not at all bad so far,' he had said to himself; 'but perhaps the Captain's taste predominated.' But when Mrs Errol came into the room, he began to think she herself might have had something to do with it. If he had not been quite a self-contained and stiff old gentleman, he would probably have started when he saw her. She looked in the simple black dress, fitting closely to her slender figure, more like a young girl than the mother of a boy of seven. She had a pretty, sorrowful young face, and a very tender, innocent look in her large brown eyes—the sorrowful look that had never quite left her face since her husband had died. Cedric was used to seeing it there; the only times he had ever seen it fade out had been when he was playing with her or talking to her, and had said some old-fashioned thing, or used some long word he had picked up out of the newspapers or in his conversations with Mr Hobbs. He was fond of using long words, and he was always pleased when they made her laugh, though he could not understand why they were laughable; they were quite serious matters with him. The lawyer's experience taught him to read people's characters very shrewdly, and as soon as he saw Cedric's mother he knew that the old Earl had made a great mistake in thinking her a vulgar, mercenary woman. Mr Havisham had never been married, he had never even been in love, but he divined that this pretty young creature with the sweet voice and sad eyes had married Captain Errol only because she loved him with all her affectionate heart, and that she had never once thought it an advantage that he was an earl's son. And he saw he should have no trouble with her, and he began to feel that perhaps little Lord Fauntleroy might not be such a trial to his noble family after all. The Captain had been a handsome fellow, and the young mother was very pretty, and perhaps the boy might be well enough to look at.

When he first told Mrs Errol what he had come for, she turned very pale.

'Oh,' she said, 'will he have to be taken away from me? We love each other so much! He is such a happiness to me! He is all I have. I have tried to be a good mother to him.' And her sweet young voice trembled, and the tears rushed into her eyes. 'You do not know what he has been to me!' she said.

The lawyer cleared his throat.

'I am obliged to tell you,' he said, 'that the Earl of Dorincourt is not—is not very friendly towards you. He is an old man, and his prejudices are very strong. He has always especially disliked America and Americans, and was very much enraged by his son's marriage. I am sorry to be the bearer of so unpleasant a communication, but he is very fixed in his determination not to see you. His plan is that Lord Fauntleroy shall be educated under his own supervision; that he shall live with him. The Earl is attached to Dorincourt Castle, and spends a great deal of time there. He is a victim to inflammatory gout, and is not fond of London. Lord Fauntleroy will, therefore, be likely to live chiefly at Dorincourt. The Earl offers to you as a home Court Lodge, which is situated pleasantly, and is not very far from the Castle. He also offers you a suitable income. Lord Fauntleroy will be permitted to visit you; the only stipulation is, that you shall not visit him or enter the park gates. You see you will not be really separated from your son, and I assure you, madam, the terms are not so harsh as—as they might have been. The advantage of such surroundings and education as Lord Fauntleroy will have, I am sure you must see, will be very great.'

He felt a little uneasy lest she should begin to cry or make a scene, as he knew some women would have done. It embarrassed and annoyed him to see women cry.

But she did not. She went to the window and stood with her face turned away for a few moments, and he saw she was trying to steady herself.

'Captain Errol was very fond of Dorincourt,' she said at last. 'He loved England, and everything English. It was always a grief to him that he was parted from his home. He was proud of his home, and of his name. He would wish—I know he would wish—that his son should know the beautiful old places, and be brought up in such a way as would be suitable to his future position.'

Then she came back to the table and stood looking up at Mr Havisham very gently.

'My husband would wish it,' she said. 'It will be best for my little boy. I know—I am sure the Earl would not be so unkind as to try to teach him not to love me; and I know— even if he tried—that my little boy is too much like his father to be harmed. He has a warm, faithful nature, and a true heart. He would love me even if he did not see me; and so long as we may see each other I ought not to suffer very much.'

'She thinks very little of herself,' the lawyer thought. 'She does not make any terms for herself.'

'Madam,' he said aloud, 'I respect your consideration for your son. He will thank you for it when he is a man. I assure you Lord Fauntleroy will be most carefully guarded, and every effort will be used to ensure his happiness. The Earl of Dorincourt will be as anxious for his comfort and well-being as you yourself could be.'

'I hope,' said the tender little mother, in a rather broken voice, 'that his grandfather will love Ceddie. The little boy has a very affectionate nature; and he has always been loved.'

Mr Havisham cleared his throat again. He could not quite imagine the gouty, fiery-tempered old Earl loving anyone very much; but he knew it would be to his interest to be kind, in his irritable way, to the child who was to be his heir. He knew too that if Ceddie were at all a credit to his name, his grandfather would be proud of him.

'Lord Fauntleroy will be comfortable, I am sure,' he replied. 'It was with a view to his happiness that the Earl desired that you should be near enough to him to see him frequently.'

He did not think it would be discreet to repeat the exact words the Earl had used, which were in fact neither polite nor amiable.

Mr Havisham preferred to express his noble patron's offer in smoother and more courteous language.

He had another slight shock when Mrs Errol asked Mary to find her little boy and bring him to her, and Mary told her where he was.

'Sure I'll foind him aisy enough, ma'am,' she said; 'for it's wid Mr Hobbs he is this minnit, settin' in his high shtool by the counther an' talkin' polytics, most loikely, or enj'yin' hisself among the soap an' candles an' pertaties, as sinsible an' shwate as ye plase.'

'Mr Hobbs has known him all his life,' Mrs Errol said to the lawyer. 'He is very kind to Ceddie, and there is a great friendship between them.'

Remembering the glimpse he had caught of the store as he passed it, and having a recollection of the barrels of potatoes and apples and the various odds and ends, Mr Havisham felt his doubts arise again. In England gentlemen's sons did not make friends of grocery-men, and it seemed to him a rather singular proceeding. It would be very awkward if the child had bad manners and a disposition to like low company. One of the bitterest humiliations of the old Earl's life had been that his two elder sons had been fond of low company. Could it be, he thought, that this boy shared their bad qualities instead of his father's good qualities.

He was thinking uneasily about this as he talked to Mrs Errol until the child came into the room. When the door opened he actually hesitated a moment before looking at

Cedric. It would perhaps have seemed very queer to a great
many people who knew him, if they could have known the
curious sensations that passed through Mr Havisham when
he looked down at the boy, who ran into his mother's arms.
He experienced a revulsion of feeling which was quite exciting. He recognized in an instant that here was one of the
finest and handsomest little fellows he had ever seen. His
beauty was something unusual. He had a strong, lithe, graceful little body and a manly little face; he held his childish head
up, and carried himself with quite a brave little air; he was so like
his father that it was really startling; he had his father's
golden hair and his mother's brown eyes, but there was
nothing sorrowful or timid in them. They were innocently
fearless eyes; he looked as if he had never feared or doubted
anything in his life.

'He is the best-bred-looking and handsomest little fellow
I ever saw,' was what Mr Havisham thought. What he said
aloud was simply: 'And so this is little Lord Fauntleroy.'

And after this the more he saw of little Lord Fauntleroy
the more of a surprise he found him. He knew very little
about children, though he had seen plenty of them in England—
fine, handsome, rosy girls and boys, who were strictly taken
care of by their tutors and governesses, and who were sometimes shy, and sometimes a trifle boisterous, but never very
interesting to a ceremonious, rigid old lawyer. Perhaps his
personal interest in little Lord Fauntleroy's fortunes made him
notice Ceddie more than he had noticed other children; but,
however that was, he certainly found himself noticing him a
great deal.

Cedric did not know he was being observed, and he only
behaved himself in his ordinary manner. He shook hands with
Mr Havisham in his friendly way when they were introduced
to each other, and he answered all his questions with the
unhesitating readiness with which he answered Mr Hobbs. He
was neither shy nor bold, and when Mr Havisham was talking
to his mother, the lawyer noticed that he listened to the

conversation with as much interest as if he had been quite grown up.

'He seems to be a very mature little fellow,' Mr Havisham said to the mother.

'I think he is, in some things,' she answered. 'He has always been very quick to learn, and he has lived a great deal with grown-up people. He has a funny little habit of using long words and expressions he has read in books, or has heard others use, but he is very fond of childish play. I think he is rather clever, but he is a very boyish little boy sometimes.'

The next time Mr Havisham met him he saw that this last was quite true. As his coupé turned the corner he caught sight of a small group of small boys, who were evidently much excited. Two of them were about to run a race, and one of them was his young lordship, and he was shouting and making as much noise as the noisiest of his companions. He stood side by side with another boy, one little red leg advanced a step.

'One to make ready!' yelled the starter. 'Two to be steady. Three—and away!'

Mr Havisham found himself leaning out of the window of his coupé with a curious feeling of interest. He really never remembered having seen anything quite like the way in which his lordship's lordly little red legs flew up behind his knicker-bockers and tore over the ground as he shot out in the race at the signal word. He shut his small hands and set his face against the wind; his bright hair streamed out behind.

'Hooray, Ced Errol!' all the boys shouted, dancing and shrieking with excitement. 'Hooray, Billy Williams! Hooray, Ceddie! Hooray, Billy! Hooray! 'Ray! 'Ray!'

'I really believe he is going to win,' said Mr Havisham. The way in which the red legs flew and flashed up and down, the shrieks of the boys, the wild efforts of Billy Williams whose brown legs were not to be despised as they followed closely in the rear of the red legs, made him feel some excitement. 'I really—I really can't help hoping he will win!' he said, with an apologetic sort of cough.

At that moment the wildest yell of all went up from the dancing, hopping boys. With one last frantic leap the future Earl of Dorincourt had reached the lamp-post at the end of the block and touched it, just two seconds before Billy Williams flung himself at it panting.

'Three cheers for Ceddie Errol!' yelled the little boys. 'Hooray for Ceddie Errol!'

Mr Havisham drew his head in at the window of his coupé and leaned back with a dry smile.

'Bravo, Lord Fauntleroy!' he said.

As his carriage stopped before the door of Mrs Errol's house, the victor and the vanquished were coming towards it, attended by the clamouring crew. Cedric walked by Billy Williams and was speaking to him. His elated little face was very red, his curls clung to his hot, moist forehead, his hands were in his pockets.

'You see,' he was saying, evidently with the intention of making defeat easy for his unsuccessful rival, 'I guess I won because my legs are a little longer than yours. I guess that was it. You see, I'm three days older than you, and that gives me a 'vantage. I'm three days older.'

And this view of the case seemed to cheer Billy Williams so much that he began to smile on the world again, and felt able to swagger a little, almost as if he had won the race instead of losing it. Somehow Ceddie Errol had a way of making people feel comfortable. Even in the first flush of his triumphs, he remembered that the person who was beaten might not feel so gay as he did, and might like to think that he *might* have been the winner under different circumstances.

That morning Mr Havisham had quite a long conversation with the winner of the race—a conversation which made him smile his dry smile, and rub his chin with his bony hand several times.

Mrs Errol had been called out of the parlour, and the lawyer and Cedric were left together. At first Mr Havisham wondered what he should say to his small companion. He had an idea that perhaps it would be best to say several things which might prepare Cedric for meeting his grandfather, and perhaps for the great change that was to come to him. He could see that Cedric had not the least idea of the sort of thing he was to see when he reached England, or the sort of home that waited for him there. He did not even know yet that his mother was not to live in the same house with him. They had thought it best to let him get over the first shock before telling him.

Mr Havisham sat in an armchair on one side of the open window; on the other side was another still larger chair, and Cedric sat in that and looked at Mr Havisham. He sat well back in the depths of his big seat, his curly head against the cushioned back, his legs crossed and his hands thrust deep into his pockets, in a quite Mr Hobbs-like way. He had been watching Mr Havisham very steadily when his mamma had been in the room, and after she was gone he still looked at him in respectful thoughtfulness. There was a short silence after Mrs Errol went out, and Cedric seemed to be studying Mr Havisham, and Mr Havisham was certainly studying Cedric. He could not make up his mind as to what an elderly gentleman should say to a little boy who won races, and wore short knickerbockers and red stockings on legs which were not long enough to hang over a big chair when he sat well back in it.

But Cedric relieved him by suddenly beginning the conversation himself.

'Do you know,' he said, 'I don't know what an earl is?'

'Don't you?' said Mr Havisham.

'No,' replied Ceddie. 'And I think when a boy is going to be one he ought to know. Don't you?'

'Well—yes,' answered Mr Havisham.

'Would you mind,' said Ceddie respectfully, 'would you mind 'splaining it to me?' (Sometimes when he used his long words he did not pronounce them quite correctly.) 'What made him an earl?'

'A king or queen in the first place,' said Mr Havisham. 'Generally he is made an earl because he has done some service to his sovereign, or some great deed.'

'Oh,' said Cedric; 'that's like the President.'

'Is it?' said Mr Havisham. 'Is that why your presidents are elected?'

'Yes,' answered Ceddie cheerfully. 'When a man is very good and knows a great deal, he is elected president. They have torch-light processions and bands, and everybody makes speeches. I used to think I might perhaps be a president, but I never thought of being an earl. I didn't know about earls,' he said rather hastily, lest Mr Havisham might feel it impolite in him not to have wished to be one. 'If I'd known about them, I dare say I should have thought I should like to be one.'

'It is rather different from being a president,' said Mr Havisham.

'Is it?' asked Cedric. 'How? Are there no torch-light processions?'

Mr Havisham crossed his own legs and put the tips of his fingers carefully together. He thought perhaps the time had come to explain matters rather more clearly.

'An earl is—is a very important person,' he began.

'So is a president!' put in Ceddie. 'The torch-light processions are five miles long, and they shoot up rockets, and the band plays! Mr Hobbs took me to see them.'

'An earl,' Mr Havisham went on, feeling rather uncertain of his ground, 'is frequently of very ancient lineage—'

'What's that?' asked Ceddie.

'Of very old family—extremely old.'

'Ah,' said Cedric, thrusting his hands deeper into his pockets. 'I suppose that is the way with the apple-woman near the park. I dare say she is of ancient lin-lenage. She is so old it would surprise you how she can stand up. She's a hundred, I should think, and yet she is out there when it rains even. I'm sorry for her, and so are the other boys. Billy Williams once had nearly a dollar, and I asked him to buy five cents' worth of apples from her every day until he had spent it all. That made twenty days, and he grew tired of apples after a week; but then—it was quite fortunate—a gentleman gave me fifty cents and I bought apples from her instead. You feel sorry for anyone that's so poor and has such ancient lin-lenage. She says hers has gone into her bones and the rain makes it worse.'

Mr Havisham felt rather at a loss as he looked at his companion's innocent, serious little face.

'I am afraid you did not quite understand me,' he explained. 'When I said "ancient lineage" I did not mean old age; I meant that the name of such a family has been known in the world a long time; perhaps for hundreds of years persons bearing that name have been known and spoken of in the history of their country.'

'Like George Washington,' said Ceddie. 'I've heard of him ever since I was born, and he was known about long before that. Mr Hobbs says he will never be forgotten. That's because of the Declaration of Independence, you know, and the Fourth of July. You see, he was a very brave man.'

'The first Earl of Dorincourt,' said Mr Havisham solemnly, 'was created an earl four hundred years ago.'

'Well, well!' said Ceddie. 'That was a long time ago! Did you tell Dearest that? It would in'trust her very much. We'll tell her when she comes in. She always likes to hear cur'us things. What else does an earl do besides being created?'

'A great many of them have helped to govern England. Some of them have been brave men and have fought in great battles in the old days.'

'I should like to do that myself,' said Cedric. 'My papa was a soldier, and he was a very brave man—as brave as George Washington. Perhaps that was because he would have been an earl if he hadn't died. I am glad earls are brave. That's a great 'vantage—to be a brave man. Once I used to be rather afraid of things—in the dark, you know; but when I thought about the soldiers in the Revolution and George Washington—it cured me.'

'There is another advantage in being an earl sometimes,' said Mr Havisham slowly, and he fixed his shrewd eyes on the little boy with a rather curious expression. 'Some earls have a great deal of money.'

He was curious because he wondered if his young friend knew what the power of money was.

'That's a good thing to have,' said Ceddie innocently. 'I wish I had a great deal of money.'

'Do you?' said Mr Havisham. 'And why?'

'Well,' explained Cedric, 'there are so many things a person can do with money. You see, there's the apple-woman. If I were very rich I should buy her a little tent to put her stall in, and a little stove, and then I should give her a dollar every morning it rained, so that she could afford to stay at home. And then—oh! I'd give her a shawl. And, you see, her bones wouldn't feel so badly. Her bones are not like our bones, they hurt her when she moves. It's very painful when your bones hurt you. If I were rich enough to do all those things for her I guess her bones would be all right.'

'Ahem!' said Mr Havisham. 'And what else would you do if you were rich?'

'Oh, I'd do a great many things. Of course I should buy Dearest all sorts of beautiful things, needle-books and fans and gold thimbles and rings, and an encyclopaedia, and a carriage, so that she needn't have to wait for the street-cars. If she liked pink silk dresses, I should buy her some, but she likes black best. But I'd take her to the big stores, and tell her to look round and choose for herself. And then Dick—'

'Who is Dick?' asked Mr Havisham.

'Dick is a boot-black,' said his young lordship, quite warming up in his interest in plans so exciting. 'He is one of the nicest boot-blacks you ever knew. He stands at the corner of a street down town. I've known him for years. Once when I was very little I was walking out with Dearest and she bought me a beautiful ball that bounced, and I was carrying it and it bounced into the middle of the street where the carriages and horses were, and I was so disappointed I began to cry—I was very little. I had kilts on, and Dick was blacking a man's shoes, and he said "Hallo!" and he ran in between the horses and caught the ball for me and wiped it off with his coat and gave it to me and said: "It's all right, young'un." So Dearest admired him very much, and so did I, and ever since then, when we go down town, we talk to him. He says "Hallo!" and I say "Hallo!" and then we talk a little, and he tells me how trade is. It's been bad lately.'

'And what would you like to do for him?' inquired the lawyer, rubbing his chin and smiling a queer smile.

'Well,' said Lord Fauntleroy, settling himself in his chair with a business air, 'I'd buy Jake out.'

'And who is Jake?' Mr Havisham said.

'He's Dick's partner, and he is the worst partner a fellow could have! Dick says so. He isn't a credit to the business, and he isn't square. He cheats, and that makes Dick mad. It would make you mad, you know, if you were blacking boots as hard as you could, and being square all the time, and your partner wasn't square at all. People like Dick, but they don't like Jake, and so sometimes they don't come twice. So if I were rich, I'd buy Jake out and get Dick a "boss" sign—he says a "boss" sign goes a long way; and I'd get him some new clothes and new brushes, and start him out fair. He says all he wants is to start out fair.'

There could have been nothing more confiding and innocent than the way in which his small lordship told his little story, quoting his friend Dick's bits of slang in the most candid good faith. He seemed to feel not a shade of a doubt that his elderly companion would be just as interested as he was himself. And in truth Mr Havisham was beginning to be greatly interested; but perhaps not quite so much in Dick and the apple-woman as in this kind little lordling, whose curly head was so busy, under its yellow thatch, with good-natured plans for his friends, and who seemed somehow to have forgotten himself altogether.

'Is there anything—' he began. 'What would you get for yourself if you were rich?'

'Lots of things!' answered Lord Fauntleroy briskly; 'but first I'd give Mary some money for Bridget—that's her sister, with twelve children and a husband out of work. She comes here and cries, and Dearest gives her things in a basket, and then she cries again, and says: "Blessin's be on yez, for a beautiful lady." And I think Mr Hobbs would like a gold watch and chain to remember me by, and a meerschaum pipe. And then I'd like to get up a company.'

'A company!' exclaimed Mr Havisham.

'Like a Republican rally,' explained Cedric, becoming quite excited. 'I'd have torches and uniforms and things for all the boys, and myself too. And we'd march, you know, and drill. That's what I'd like for myself, if I were rich.'

The door opened and Mrs Errol came in.

'I am sorry to have been obliged to leave you so long,' she said to Mr Havisham, 'but a poor woman, who is in great trouble, came to see me.'

'This young gentleman,' said Mr Havisham, 'has been telling me about some of his friends, and what he would do for them if he were rich.'

'Bridget is one of his friends,' said Mrs Errol; 'and it is Bridget to whom I have been talking in the kitchen. She is in great trouble now because her husband has rheumatic fever.'

Cedric slipped down out of his big chair.

'I think I'll go and see her,' he said, 'and ask her how he is. He's a nice man when he is well. I'm obliged to him because he once made me a sword out of wood. He's a very talented man.'

He ran out of the room, and Mr Havisham rose from his chair. He seemed to have something in his mind which he wished to speak of. He hesitated a moment, and then said, looking down at Mrs Errol:

'Before I left Dorincourt Castle I had an interview with the Earl, in which he gave me some instructions. He is desirous that his grandson should look forward with some pleasure to his future life in England, and also to his acquaintance with himself. He said that I must let his lordship know that the change in his life would bring him money and the pleasures children enjoy; if he expressed any wishes I was to gratify them, and to tell him that his grandfather had given him what he wished. I am aware that the Earl did not expect

anything quite like this; but if it would give Lord Fauntleroy
pleasure to assist this poor woman, I should feel that the Earl
would be displeased if he were not gratified.'

For the second time he did not repeat the Earl's exact
words. His lordship had indeed said:

'Make the lad understand that I can give him anything he
wants. Let him know what it is to be the grandson of the Earl
of Dorincourt. Buy him everything he takes a fancy to: let
him have money in his pockets, and tell him his grandfather
put it there.'

His motives were far from being good, and if he had
been dealing with a nature less affectionate and warm-hearted
than little Lord Fauntleroy's, great harm might have been
done. And Cedric's mother was too gentle to suspect any
harm. She thought that perhaps this meant that a lonely,
unhappy old man, whose children were dead, wished to be
kind to her little boy, and win his love and confidence. And it
pleased her very much to think that Ceddie would be able to
help Bridget. It made her happier to know that the very first
result of the strange fortune which had befallen her little boy
was that he could do kind things for those who needed
kindness. Quite a warm colour bloomed on her pretty young
face.

'Oh,' she said, 'that was very kind of the Earl; Cedric
will be so glad! He has always been fond of Bridget and
Michael. They are quite deserving. I have often wished I had
been able to help them more. Michael is a hard-working man
when he is well, but he has been ill a long time and needs
expensive medicines and warm clothing and nourishing food.
He and Bridget will not be wasteful of what is given them.'

Mr Havisham put his thin hand in his breast pocket and
drew forth a large pocket-book. There was a queer look in his
keen face. The truth was he was wondering what the Earl of
Dorincourt would say when he was told what was the first
wish of his grandson that had been granted. He wondered
what the cross, worldly, selfish old nobleman would think of
it.

'I do not know that you have realized,' he said, 'that the Earl of Dorincourt is an exceedingly rich man. He can afford to gratify any caprice. I think it would please him to know that Lord Fauntleroy had been indulged in any fancy. If you will call him back and allow me, I shall give him five pounds for these people.'

'That would be twenty-five dollars!' exclaimed Mrs Errol. 'It will seem like wealth to them. I can scarcely believe that it is true.'

'It is quite true,' said Mr Havisham with his dry smile. 'A great change has taken place in your son's life, a great deal of power will lie in his hands.'

'Oh,' cried his mother. 'And he is such a little boy—a very little boy. How can I teach him to use it well? It makes me half afraid. My pretty little Ceddie!'

The lawyer slightly cleared his throat. It touched his worldly, hard old heart to see the tender, timid look in her brown eyes.

'I think, madam,' he said, 'that if I may judge from my interview with Lord Fauntleroy this morning, the next Earl of Dorincourt will think for others as well as for his noble self. He is only a child yet, but I think he may be trusted.'

Then his mother went for Cedric and brought him back into the parlour. Mr Havisham heard him talking before he entered the room.

'It's infam-natory rheumatism,' he was saying, 'and that's a kind of rheumatism that's dreadful. And he thinks about the rent not being paid, and Bridget says that makes the inf'ammation worse. And Pat could get a place in a store if he had some clothes.'

His little face looked quite anxious when he came in. He was very sorry for Bridget.

'Dearest said you wanted me,' he said to Mr Havisham. 'I've been talking to Bridget.'

Mr Havisham looked down at him a moment. He felt a little awkward and undecided. As Cedric's mother had said, he was a very little boy.

'The Earl of Dorincourt—' he began, and then he glanced involuntarily at Mrs Errol.

Little Lord Fauntleroy's mother suddenly kneeled down by him and put her tender arms around his childish body.

'Ceddie,' she said, 'the Earl is your grandpapa, your own papa's father. He is very, very kind, and he loves you and wishes you to love him, because the sons who were his little boys are dead. He wishes you to be happy and to make other people happy. He is very rich, and he wishes you to have everything you would like to have. He told Mr Havisham so, and gave him a great deal of money for you. You can give some to Bridget now; enough to pay her rent and buy Michael everything. Isn't that fine, Ceddie? Isn't he good?' And she kissed the child on his round cheek, where the bright colour suddenly flashed up in his excited amazement.

He looked from his mother to Mr Havisham.

'Can I have it now?' he cried. 'Can I give it to her this minute? She's just going.'

Mr Havisham handed him the money. It was in fresh clean greenbacks and made a neat roll.

Ceddie flew out of the room.

'Bridget!' they heard him shout, as he tore into the kitchen. 'Bridget, wait a minute! Here's some money. It's for you, and you can pay the rent. My grandpapa gave it to me. It's for you and Michael!'

'Oh, Master Ceddie!' cried Bridget, in an awe-stricken voice. 'It's twenty-foive dollars is here. Where be's the misthress?'

'I think I shall have to go and explain it to her,' Mrs Errol said.

So she too went out of the room, and Mr Havisham was left alone for a while. He went to the window and stood looking out into the street reflectively. He was thinking of the old Earl of Dorincourt, sitting in his great, splendid, gloomy library at the castle, gouty and lonely, surrounded by grandeur and luxury, but not really loved by anyone, because in all his long life he had never really loved anyone but himself;

he had been selfish and self-indulgent, and arrogant and passionate; he had cared so much for the Earl of Dorincourt and his pleasures that there had been no time for him to think of other people; all his wealth and power, all the benefits from his noble name and high rank, had seemed to him to be things only to be used to amuse and give pleasure to the Earl of Dorincourt; and now that he was an old man, all this excitement and self-indulgence had only brought him ill-health and irritability and a dislike of the world, which certainly disliked him. In spite of all his splendour, there was never a more unpopular old nobleman than the Earl of Dorincourt, and there could scarcely have been a more lonely one. He could fill his castle with guests if he chose. He could give great dinners and splendid hunting parties; but he knew that in secret the people who would accept his invitations were afraid of his frowning old face and sarcastic, biting speeches. He had a cruel tongue and a bitter nature, and he took pleasure in sneering at people and making them feel uncomfortable, when he had the power to do so, because they were sensitive or proud or timid.

Mr Havisham knew his hard, fierce ways by heart, and he was thinking of him as he looked out of the window into the quiet, narrow street. And there rose in his mind, in sharp contrast, the picture of the cheery, handsome little fellow sitting in the big chair and telling his story of his friends, Dick and the apple-woman, in his generous, innocent, honest way. And he thought of the immense income, the beautiful, majestic estates, the wealth, and power for good or evil, which in the course of time would lie in the small, chubby hands little Lord Fauntleroy thrust so deep into his pockets.

'It will make a great difference,' he said to himself. 'It will make a great difference.'

Cedric and his mother came back soon after. Cedric was in high spirits. He sat down in his own chair, between his mother and the lawyer, and fell into one of his quaint attitudes, with his hands on his knees. He was glowing with enjoyment of Bridget's relief and rapture.

'She cried!' he said. 'She said she was crying for joy. I never saw anyone cry for joy before. My grandpapa must be a very good man. I didn't know he was so good a man. It's more—more agreeabler to be an earl than I thought it was. I'm almost glad—I'm almost *quite* glad I'm going to be one.'

THREE

Leaving Home

Cedric's good opinion of the advantages of being an earl increased greatly during the next week. It seemed almost impossible for him to realize that there was scarcely anything he might wish to do which he could not do easily; in fact I think it may be said that he did not fully realize it at all. But at least he understood, after a few conversations with Mr Havisham, that he could gratify all his nearest wishes, and he proceeded to gratify them with a simplicity and delight which caused Mr Havisham much diversion. In the week before they sailed for England he did many curious things. The lawyer long after remembered the morning they went down together to pay a visit to Dick, and the afternoon they so amazed the apple-woman of ancient lineage by stopping before her stall and telling her she was to have a tent and a stove and a shawl and a sum of money, which seemed to her quite wonderful.

'For I have to go to England and be a lord,' explained Cedric sweet-temperedly. 'And I shouldn't like to have your bones on my mind every time it rained. My own bones never hurt, so I think I don't know how painful a person's bones can be, but I've sympathized with you a great deal, and I hope you'll be better.

'She's a very good apple-woman,' he said to Mr Havisham

35

as they walked away, leaving the proprietress of the stall almost gasping for breath, and not at all believing in her great fortune. 'Once, when I fell down and cut my knee, she gave me an apple for nothing. I've always remembered her for it. You know you always remember people who are kind to you.'

It had never occurred to his honest, simple, little mind that there were people who could forget kindnesses.

The interview with Dick was quite exciting. Dick had just been having a great deal of trouble with Jake, and was in low spirits when they saw him. His amazement when Cedric calmly announced that they had come to give him what seemed a very great thing to him, and would set all his troubles right, almost struck him dumb. Lord Fauntleroy's manner of announcing the object of his visit was very simple and unceremonious. Mr Havisham was much impressed by its directness as he stood by and listened. The statement that his old friend had become a lord, and was in danger of being an earl if he lived long enough, caused Dick to so open his eyes and mouth, and start, that his cap fell off. When he picked it up he uttered a rather singular exclamation. Mr Havisham thought it singular, but Cedric had heard it before.

'I soy!' he said, 'what're yer givin' us?' This plainly embarrassed his lordship a little, but he bore himself bravely.

'Everybody thinks it not true at first,' he said. 'Mr Hobbs thought I'd had a sunstroke. I didn't think I was going to like it myself, but I like it better now I'm used to it. The one who is the earl now—he's my grandpapa; and he wants me to do anything I like. He's very kind, if he *is* an earl; and he sent me a lot of money by Mr Havisham, and I've brought some to you to buy Jake out.'

And the end of the matter was that Dick actually bought Jake out, and found himself the possessor of the business, and some new brushes and a most astonishing sign and outfit. He could not believe in his good luck any more easily than the apple-woman of ancient lineage could believe in hers; he walked about like a boot-black in a dream; he stared at his young benefactor and felt as if he might wake up at any moment. He scarcely seemed to realize anything until Cedric put out his hand to shake hands with him before going away.

'Well, good-bye,' he said; and though he tried to speak steadily, there was a little trouble in his voice and he winked his big brown eyes. 'And I hope trade'll be good. I'm sorry I'm going away to leave you, but perhaps I shall come back again when I'm an earl. And I wish you'd write to me, because we were always good friends. And if you write to me, here's where you must send your letter.' And he gave him a slip of paper. 'And my name isn't Cedric Errol any more; it's Lord Fauntleroy and—and good-bye, Dick.'

Dick winked his eyes also, and yet they looked rather moist about the lashes. He was not an educated boot-black, and he would have felt it difficult to tell what he felt just then, if he had tried; perhaps that was why he didn't try, and only winked his eyes and swallowed a lump in his throat.

'I wish ye wasn't goin' away,' he said in a husky voice. Then he winked his eyes again. Then he looked at Mr Havisham and touched his cap. 'Thanky, sir, fur bringin' him down here an' fur wot ye've done. He's—he's a queer little feller,' he added. 'I've allers thort a heap of him. He's such a game little feller, an'—an' such a queer little 'un.'

And when they turned away he stood and looked after them in a dazed kind of way, and there was still a mist in his eyes and a lump in his throat, as he watched the gallant little figure marching gaily along by the side of its tall, rigid escort.

Until the day of his departure his lordship spent as much time as possible with Mr Hobbs in the store. Gloom had settled upon Mr Hobbs; he was much depressed in spirits. When his young friend brought to him in triumph the parting gift of a gold watch and chain, Mr Hobbs found it difficult to acknowledge it properly. He laid the case on his stout knee, and blew his nose violently several times.

'There's something written on it,' said Cedric, 'inside the case. I told the man myself what to say. ''From his oldest friend, Lord Fauntleroy, to Mr Hobbs. When this you see, remember me.'' I don't want you to forget me.'

Mr Hobbs blew his nose very loudly again.

'I shan't forget you,' he said, speaking a trifle huskily, as Dick had spoken; 'nor don't you go and forget me when you get among the British arrystocracy.'

'I shouldn't forget you whoever I was among,' answered his lordship. 'I've spent my happiest hours with you; at least, some of my happiest hours. I hope you'll come to see me some time. I'm sure grandpapa would be very much pleased. Perhaps he'll write and ask you when I tell him about you? You—you wouldn't mind his being an earl, would you? I mean you wouldn't stay away just because he was one, if he invited you to come?'

'I'd come to see you,' replied Mr Hobbs graciously.

So it seemed to be agreed that if he received a pressing invitation from the Earl to come and spend a few months at Dorincourt Castle, he was to lay aside his republican prejudices and pack his valise at once.

At last the preparations were complete; the day came when the trunks were taken to the steamer, and the hour arrived when the carriage stood at the door. Then a curious feeling of loneliness came upon the little boy. His mamma had been shut up in her room for some time; when she came down the stairs her eyes looked large and wet, and her sweet mouth was trembling. Cedric went to her, and she bent down to him, and he put his arms around her, and they kissed each other. He knew something made them both sorry, though he scarcely knew what it was; but one tender little thought rose to his lips.

'We liked this little house, Dearest, didn't we?' he said. 'We always will like it, won't we?'

'Yes—yes,' she answered in a low, sweet voice. 'Yes, darling.'

And then they went into the carriage and Cedric sat very close to her, and as she looked back out of the window he looked at her, and stroked her hand and held it close.

And then, it seemed almost directly, they were on the steamer in the midst of the wildest bustle and confusion; carriages were driving down and leaving passengers; passengers were getting into a state of excitement about baggage which had not arrived and threatened to be too late; big trunks and cases were being bumped down and dragged about; sailors were uncoiling ropes and hurrying to and fro; officers were giving orders; ladies and gentlemen and children and nurses were coming on board—some were laughing and looked gay, some were silent and sad, here and there two or three were crying and touching their eyes with their handkerchiefs. Cedric found something to interest him on every side; he looked at the piles of rope, at the furled sails, at the tall, tall masts which seemed almost to touch the hot blue sky; he began to make plans for conversing with the sailors and gaining some information on the subject of pirates.

It was just at the very last, when he was standing leaning on the railing of the upper deck and watching the final preparations, enjoying the excitement and the shouts of the sailors and wharfmen, that his attention was called to a slight bustle in one of the groups not far from him. Someone was hurriedly forcing his way through this group and coming towards him. It was a boy, with something red in his hand. It was Dick. He came up to Cedric quite breathless.

'I've run all the way,' he said. 'I've come down to see ye off. Trade's been prime! I bought this for ye out o' what I made yesterday. Ye kin wear it when ye get among the swells. I lost the paper when I was tryin' to get through them fellers downstairs. They didn't want to let me up. It's a handkercher.'

He poured it all forth as if in one sentence. A bell rang and he made a leap away before Cedric had time to speak.

'Good-bye!' he panted. 'Wear it when ye get among the swells.' And he darted off and was gone.

A few seconds later they saw him struggle through the crowd on the lower deck, and rush on shore just before the gang-plank was drawn in. He stood on the wharf and waved his cap.

Cedric held the handkerchief in his hand. It was of bright red silk, ornamented with purple horseshoes and horses' heads.

There was a great straining and creaking and confusion. The people on the wharf began to shout to their friends, and the people on the steamer shouted back:

'Good-bye! Good-bye! Good-bye, old fellow!' Everyone seemed to be saying: 'Don't forget us. Write when you get to Liverpool. Good-bye! Good-bye!'

Little Lord Fauntleroy leaned forward and waved the red handkerchief.

'Good-bye, Dick!' he shouted lustily. 'Thank you! Good-bye, Dick!'

And the big steamer moved away, and the people cheered again, and Cedric's mother drew the veil over her eyes, and on the shore there was left great confusion; but Dick saw nothing save the bright, childish face and the bright hair that the sun shone on and the breeze lifted, and he heard nothing but the hearty childish voice calling 'Good-bye, Dick!' as little Lord Fauntleroy steamed slowly away from the home of his birth to the unknown land of his ancestors.

FOUR

In England

It was during the voyage that Cedric's mother told him that his home was not to be hers; and when he first understood it his grief was so great that Mr Havisham saw that the Earl had been wise in making the arrangements that his mother should be quite near him, and see him often; for it was very plain he could not have borne the separation otherwise. But his mother managed the little fellow so sweetly and lovingly, and made him feel she would be so near him, that after a while he ceased to be oppressed by the fear of any real parting.

'My house is not far from the Castle, Ceddie,' she repeated each time the subject was referred to—'a very little way from yours, and you can always run in and see me every day, and you will have so many things to tell me, and we shall be so happy together! It is a beautiful place. Your papa has often told me about it. He loved it very much; and you will love it too.'

'I should love it better if you were there,' his small lordship said with a heavy little sigh.

He could not but feel puzzled by so strange a state of affairs, which could put his 'Dearest' in one house and himself in another.

The fact was that Mrs Errol had thought it better not to tell him why this plan had been made.

'I should prefer he should not be told,' she said to Mr Havisham. 'He would not really understand; he would only be shocked and hurt; and I feel sure that his feeling for the Earl will be a more natural and affectionate one if he does not know that his grandfather dislikes me so bitterly. He has never seen hatred or hardness, and it would be a great blow to him to find out that anyone could hate me. He is so loving himself, and I am so dear to him! It is better for him that he should not be told until he is much older, and it is far better for the Earl. It would make a barrier between them, even though Ceddie is such a child.'

So Cedric only knew that there was some mysterious reason for the arrangement, some reason which he was not old enough to understand, but which would be explained when he was older. He was puzzled; but after all it was not the reason he cared about so much; and after many talks with his mother, in which she comforted him and placed before him the bright side of the picture, the dark side of it gradually began to fade out, though now and then Mr Havisham saw him sitting in some queer little old-fashioned attitude, watching the sea, with a very grave face, and more than once he heard an unchildish sigh rise to his lips.

'I don't like it,' he said once as he was having one of his almost venerable talks with the lawyer. 'You don't know how much I don't like it; but there are a great many troubles in this world, and you have to bear them. Mary says so, and I've heard Mr Hobbs say it too. And Dearest wants me to like to live with my grandpapa, because, you see, all his children are dead, and that's very mournful. It makes you sorry for a man when all his children have died—and one was killed suddenly.'

One of the things which always delighted the people who made the acquaintance of his young lordship was the sage little air he wore at times when he gave himself up to conversation; combined with his occasionally elderly remarks and the extreme innocence and seriousness of his round child-ish face, it was irresistible. He was such a handsome, blooming, curly-headed little fellow, that, when he sat down and nursed his knee with his chubby hands, and con-versed with much gravity, he was a source of great entertain-ment to his hearers. Gradually Mr Havisham had begun to derive a great deal of private pleasure and amusement from his society.

'And so you are going to try to like the Earl?' he said.

'Yes,' answered his lordship. 'He's my relation, and of course you have to like your relations: and besides, he's been very kind to me. When a person does so many things for you and wants you to have everything you wish for, of course you'd like him if he wasn't your relation; but when he's your relation and does that, why you're very fond of him.'

'Do you think,' suggested Mr Havisham, 'that he will be fond of you?'

'Well,' said Cedric, 'I think he will, because, you see, I'm his relation too, and I'm his boy's little boy besides, and, well, don't you see—of course he must be fond of me now, or he wouldn't want me to have everything that I like, and he wouldn't have sent you for me.'

'Oh,' remarked the lawyer, "that's it, is it?'

'Yes,' said Cedric, 'that's it. Don't you think that's it too? Of course a man would be fond of his grandson.'

The people who had been seasick had no sooner recov-ered from their seasickness, and come on deck to recline in their steamer chairs and enjoy themselves, than everyone seemed to know the romantic story of little Lord Fauntleroy, and everyone took an interest in the little fellow, who ran about the ship or walked with his mother or the tall, thin old lawyer, or talked to the sailors. Everyone liked him; he made friends everywhere. He was ever ready to make friends. When the gentlemen walked up and down the deck, and let him walk with them, he stepped out with a manly, sturdy little tramp, and answered all their jokes with much gay enjoyment; when the ladies talked to him there was always laughter in the group of which he was the centre; when he played with the children there was always magnificent fun on hand. Among the sailors he had the heartiest friends; he heard miraculous stories about pirates and shipwrecks and desert islands; he learned to splice ropes and rig toy ships, and gained an amount of information concerning 'tops'les' and 'mains'les', quite surprising. His conversations had indeed quite a nautical flavour at times, and on one occasion he raised a shout of laughter in a group of ladies and gentlemen who were sitting on deck, wrapped in shawls and overcoats, by saying sweetly, and with a very engaging expression:

'Shiver my timbers, but it's a cold day!'

It surprised him when they laughed. He had picked up this seafaring remark from an 'elderly naval man' of the name of Jerry, who told him stories in which it occurred frequently. To judge from his stories of his own adventures, Jerry had made some two or three thousand voyages, and had been invariably shipwrecked on each occasion on an island densely populated with bloodthirsty cannibals. Judging also by these same exciting adventures, he had been partially roasted and eaten frequently and had been scalped some fifteen or twenty times.

'That is why he is so bald,' explained Lord Fauntleroy to his mamma. 'After you have been scalped several times the hair never grows again. Jerry's never grew after the last time, when the King of the Parromachaweekins did it with the knife made out of the skull of the Chief of the Wopslemumpkies. He says it was one of the most serious times he ever had. He was so frightened that his hair stood right straight up when the king flourished his knife, and it never would lie down, and the king wears it that way now, and it looks something like a hairbrush. I never heard anything like the asperiences Jerry has had! I should so like to tell Mr Hobbs about them!'

Sometimes, when the weather was very disagreeable and people were kept below decks in the saloon, a party of his grown-up friends would persuade him to tell them some of these 'asperiences' of Jerry's, and, as he sat relating them with great delight and fervour, there was certainly no more popular voyager on any ocean steamer crossing the Atlantic than little Lord Fauntleroy. He was always innocently and good-naturedly ready to do his small best to add to the general entertainment, and there was a charm in the very unconsciousness of his own childish importance.

'Jerry's stories int'rust them very much,' he said to his mamma. 'For my part—you must excuse me, Dearest—but sometimes I should have thought they couldn't be all quite true, if they hadn't happened to Jerry himself; but as they all happened to Jerry—well, it's very strange, you know, and perhaps sometimes he may forget and be a little mistaken, as he's been scalped so often. Being scalped a great many times might make a person forgetful.'

It was eleven days after he had said good-bye to his friend Dick before he reached Liverpool; and it was on the night of the twelfth day that the carriage, in which he and his mother and Mr Havisham had driven from the station, stopped before the gates of Court Lodge. They could not see much of the house in the darkness. Cedric only saw that there was a carriage drive under great arching trees, and after the carriage had rolled down this carriage drive a short distance, he saw an open door and a stream of bright light coming through it.

Mary had come with them to attend her mistress, and she had reached the house before them. When Cedric jumped out of the carriage he saw one or two servants standing in the wide bright hall, and Mary stood in the doorway.

Lord Fauntleroy sprang at her with a gay little shout.

'Did you get here, Mary?' he said. 'Here's Mary, Dearest,' and he kissed the maid on her rough red cheek.

'I am glad you are here, Mary,' Mrs Errol said to her in a low voice. 'It is such a comfort to me to see you. It takes the strangeness away.' And she held out her little hand, which Mary squeezed encouragingly. She knew how this first 'strangeness' must feel to this little mother who had left her own land and was about to give up her child.

The English servants looked with curiosity at both the

boy and his mother. They had heard all sorts of rumours about them both; they knew how angry the old Earl had been, and why Mrs Errol was to live at the Lodge and her little boy at the Castle; they knew all about the great fortune he was to inherit and about the savage old grandfather and his gout and his tempers.

'He'll have no easy time of it, poor little chap,' they had said among themselves.

But they did not know what sort of a little lord had come among them; they did not quite understand the character of the next Earl of Dorincourt.

He pulled off his overcoat quite as if he were used to doing things for himself, and began to look about him. He looked about the broad hall, at the pictures and stags' antlers and curious things that ornamented it. They seemed curious to him because he had never seen such things before in a private house.

'Dearest,' he said, 'this is a very pretty house, isn't it? I am glad you are going to live here. It's quite a large house.'

It was quite a large house compared to the one in the shabby New York street, and it was very pretty and cheerful. Mary led them upstairs to a bright chintz-hung bedroom where a fire was burning, and a large snow-white Persian cat was sleeping luxuriously on the white fur hearthrug.

'It was the housekaper up at the Castle, ma'am, sint her to yez,' explained Mary. 'It's herself is a kind-hearted lady an' has had iverything done to prepar' fur yez. I seen her meself a few minnits, an' she was fond av the Capt'in, ma'am, an' graivs fur him; and she said to say the big cat slapin' on the rug moight make the room same homeloike to yez. She knowed Capt'in Errol whin he was a bye—an' a foine handsum' bye she ses he was, an' a foine young man wid a plisint word fur everyone, great an' shmall. An' ses I to her, ses I, "He's lift a bye that's loike him, ma'am, fur a foiner little felly niver sthipped in shoe-leather".'

When they were ready they went downstairs into another big bright room; its ceiling was low, and the furniture was heavy and beautifully carved, the chairs were deep and had high massive backs, and there were queer shelves and cabinets with strange, pretty ornaments on them. There was a great tiger-skin before the fire, and an armchair on each side of it. The stately white cat had responded to Lord Fauntleroy's stroking and followed him downstairs, and when he threw himself down upon the rug she curled herself up grandly beside him as if she intended to make friends. Cedric was so pleased that he put his head down by hers, and lay stroking her, not noticing what his mother and Mr Havisham were saying.

They were indeed speaking in a rather low tone. Mrs Errol looked a little pale and agitated.

'He need not go tonight?' she said. 'He will stay with me tonight?'

'Yes,' answered Mr Havisham in the same low tone; 'it will not be necessary for him to go tonight. I myself will go to the Castle as soon as we have dined, and inform the Earl of our arrival.'

Mrs Errol glanced down at Cedric. He was lying in a graceful, careless attitude upon the black-and-yellow skin; the fire shone on his handsome, flushed little face, and on the tumbled, curly hair spread out on the rug; the big cat was purring in drowsy content; she liked the caressing touch of the kind little hand on her fur.

Mrs Errol smiled faintly.

'His lordship does not know all that he is taking from me,' she said rather sadly. Then she looked at the lawyer. 'Will you tell him, if you please,' she said, 'that I should rather not have the money?'

'The money!' Mr Havisham exclaimed. 'You cannot mean the income he proposed to settle upon you?'

'Yes,' she answered quite simply; 'I think I should rather not have it. I am obliged to accept the house, and I thank him for it, because it makes it possible for me to be near my child; but I have a little money of my own—enough to live simply upon—and I should rather not take the other, as he dislikes me so much I should feel a little as if I were selling Cedric to him. I am giving him up only because I love him enough to forget myself for his good, and because his father would wish it to be so.'

Mr Havisham rubbed his chin.

'This is very strange,' he said. 'He will be very angry. He won't understand it.'

'I think he will understand it after he thinks it over,' she said. 'I do not really need the money, and why should I accept luxuries from the man who hates me so much that he takes my little boy from me—his son's child?'

Mr Havisham looked reflective for a few moments.

'I will deliver your message,' he said afterwards.

And then the dinner was brought in and they sat down together, the big cat taking a seat on a chair near Cedric's and purring majestically throughout the meal.

When, later in the evening, Mr Havisham presented himself at the Castle, he was taken at once to the Earl. He found him sitting by the fire in a luxurious easy chair, his foot on a gout-stool. He looked at the lawyer sharply from under his shaggy eyebrows, but Mr Havisham could see that, in spite of his pretence at calmness, he was nervous and secretly excited.

'Well,' he said; 'well, Havisham, come back, have you? What's the news?'

'Lord Fauntleroy and his mother are at Court Lodge,' replied Mr Havisham. 'They bore the voyage very well and are in excellent health.'

The Earl made a half-impatient sound and moved his hand restlessly.

'Glad to hear it,' he said brusquely. 'So far, so good. Make yourself comfortable. Have a glass of wine and settle down. What else?'

'His lordship remains with his mother tonight. Tomorrow I will bring him to the Castle.'

The Earl's elbow was resting on the arm of his chair; he put his hand up and shielded his eyes with it.

'Well?' he said; 'go on. You know I told you not to write to me about the matter, and I know nothing whatever about it. What kind of a lad is he? I don't care about the mother; what sort of lad is he?'

Mr Havisham drank a little of the glass of port he had poured out for himself, and sat holding it in his hand.

'It is rather difficult to judge of the character of a child of seven,' he said cautiously.

The Earl's prejudices were very intense. He looked up quickly and uttered a rough word.

'A fool, is he?' he exclaimed. 'Or a clumsy cub? His American blood tells, does it?'

'I do not think it has injured him, my lord,' replied the lawyer in his dry, deliberate fashion. 'I don't know much about children, but I thought him rather a fine lad.'

His manner of speech was always deliberate and unenthusiastic, but he made it a trifle more so than usual. He had a shrewd fancy that it would be better that the Earl should judge for himself, and be quite unprepared for his first interview with his grandson.

'Healthy and well grown?' asked my lord.

'Apparently very healthy, and quite well grown,' replied the lawyer.

'Straight-limbed and well enough to look at?' demanded the Earl.

A very slight smile touched Mr Havisham's thin lips. There rose up before his mind's eye the picture he had left at Court Lodge—the beautiful, graceful child's body lying upon the tiger-skin in careless comfort—the bright, tumbled hair spread on the rug—the bright, rosy boy's face.

'Rather a handsome boy, I think, my lord, as boys go,' he said, 'though I am scarcely a judge perhaps. But you will find him somewhat different to most English children, I dare say.'

'I haven't a doubt of that,' snarled the Earl, a twinge of gout seizing him. 'A lot of impudent little beggars, those American children; I've heard that often enough.'

'It is not exactly impudence in his case,' said Mr Havisham. 'I can scarcely describe what the difference is. He has lived more with older people than with children, and the difference seems to be a mixture of maturity and childishness.'

'American impudence!' protested the Earl. 'I've heard of it before. They call it precocity and freedom. Beastly, impudent, bad manners; that's what it is!'

Mr Havisham drank some more port. He seldom argued with his lordly patron—never when his lordly patron's noble leg was inflamed by gout. At such times it was always better to leave him alone. So there was a silence of a few moments; it was Mr Havisham who broke it.

'I have a message to deliver from Mrs Errol,' he remarked.

'I don't want any of her messages!' growled his lordship; 'the less I hear of her the better.'

'This is a rather important one,' explained the lawyer. 'She prefers not to accept the income you proposed to settle on her.'

The Earl started visibly.

'What's that?' he cried out. 'What's that?'

Mr Havisham repeated his words.

'She says it is not necessary, and that as the relations between you are not friendly—'

'Not friendly!' ejaculated my lord savagely; 'I should say they were not friendly! I hate to think of her! A mercenary, sharp-voiced American! I don't wish to see her!'

'My lord,' said Mr Havisham, 'you can scarcely call her mercenary. She has asked for nothing. She does not accept the money you offer her.'

'All done for effect!' snapped his noble lordship. 'She wants to wheedle me into seeing her. She thinks I shall admire her spirit. I don't admire it! It's only American independence! I won't have her living like a beggar at my park gates. As she's the boy's mother she has a position to keep up, and she shall keep it up. She shall have the money, whether she likes it or not!'

'She won't spend it,' said Mr Havisham.

'I don't care whether she spends it or not!' blustered my lord. 'She shall have it sent to her. She shan't tell people that she has to live like a pauper because I have done nothing for her! She wants to give the boy a bad opinion of me! I suppose she has poisoned his mind against me already!'

'No,' said Mr Havisham. 'I have another message, which will prove to you that she has not done that.'

'I don't want to hear it!' panted the Earl, out of breath with anger and excitement and gout.

But Mr Havisham delivered it.

'She asks you not to let Lord Fauntleroy hear anything which would lead him to understand that you separate him from her because of your prejudice against her. He is very fond of her, and she is convinced that it would cause a barrier to exist between you. She says he would not comprehend it and it might make him fear you in some measure, or at least cause him to feel less affection for you. She has told him that he is too young to understand the reason, but shall hear it when he is older. She wishes that there should be no shadow on your first meeting.'

The Earl sank back into his chair. His deep-set fierce old eyes gleamed under his beetling brows.

'Come, now!' he said, still breathlessly. 'Come now! You don't mean the mother hasn't told him?'

'Not one word, my lord,' replied the lawyer coolly. 'That I can assure you. The child is prepared to believe you the most amiable and affectionate of grandparents. Nothing— absolutely nothing—has been said to him to give him the slightest doubt of your perfection. And as I carried out your commands in every detail, while in New York, he certainly regards you as a wonder of generosity.'

'He does, eh?' said the Earl.

'I give you my word of honour,' said Mr Havisham, 'that Lord Fauntleroy's impressions of you will depend entirely upon yourself. And if you will pardon the liberty I take in making the suggestion, I think you will succeed better with him if you take the precaution not to speak slightingly of his mother.'

'Pooh, pooh!' said the Earl. 'The youngster's only seven years old!'

'He has spent those seven years at his mother's side,' returned Mr Havisham; 'and she has all his affection.'

FIVE

At the Castle

It was late in the afternoon when the carriage containing little Lord Fauntleroy and Mr Havisham drove up the long avenue which led to the Castle. The Earl had given orders that his grandson should arrive in time to dine with him, and for some reason best known to himself he had also ordered that the child should be sent alone into the room in which he intended to receive him. As the carriage rolled up the avenue, Lord Fauntleroy sat leaning comfortably against the luxurious cushions, and regarded the prospect with great interest. He was, in fact, interested in everything he saw. He had been interested in the carriage, with its large, splendid horses and their glittering harness; he had been interested in the tall coachman and footman, with their resplendent livery; and he had been especially interested in the coronet on the panels, and had struck up an acquaintance with the footman for the purpose of inquiring what it meant.

When the carriage reached the great gates of the park, he looked out of the window to get a good view of the huge stone lions ornamenting the entrance. The gates were opened by a motherly, rosy-looking woman, who came out of a pretty ivy-covered lodge. Two children ran out of the house and stood looking with round wide-open eyes at the little boy in the carriage, who looked at them also. Their mother stood curtsying and smiling, and the children, on receiving a sign from her, made bobbing little curtsies too.

'Does she know me?' asked Lord Fauntleroy. 'I think she must think she knows me.' And he took off his black velvet cap to her and smiled.

'How do you do?' he said brightly. 'Good afternoon!'

The woman seemed pleased, he thought. The smile broadened on her rosy face and a kind look came into her blue eyes.

'God bless your lordship!' she said. 'God bless your pretty face! Good luck and happiness to your lordship! Welcome to you!'

Lord Fauntleroy waved his cap and nodded to her again as the carriage rolled by her.

'I like that woman,' he said. 'She looks as if she liked boys. I should like to come here and play with her children. I wonder if she has enough to make up a company?'

Mr Havisham did not tell him that he would scarcely be allowed to make playmates of the gate-keeper's children. The lawyer thought there was time enough for giving him that information.

The carriage rolled on and on between the great beautiful trees which grew on each side of the avenue and stretched their broad swaying branches in an arch across it. Cedric had never seen such trees, they were so grand and stately, and their branches grew so low down on their huge trunks. He did not then know that Dorincourt Castle was one of the most beautiful in all England; that its park was one of the broadest and finest, and its trees and avenue almost without rivals. But he did know that it was all very beautiful. He liked the big, broad-branched trees, with the late afternoon sunlight striking golden lances through them. He liked the perfect stillness which rested on everything. He felt a great, strange pleasure in the beauty of which he caught glimpses under and between the sweeping boughs—the great, beautiful spaces of the park, with still other trees, standing sometimes stately and alone, and sometimes in groups. Now and then they passed places where tall ferns grew in masses, and again and again the ground was azure with the bluebells swaying in the soft breeze. Several times he started up with a laugh of delight as a rabbit leaped up from under the greenery and scudded away with a twinkle of short white tail behind it. Once a covey of partridges rose with a sudden whir and flew away, and then he shouted and clapped his hands.

'It's a beautiful place, isn't it?' he said to Mr Havisham. 'I never saw such a beautiful place. It's prettier even than Central Park.'

He was rather puzzled by the length of time they were on their way.

'How far is it,' he said at length, 'from the gate to the front door?'

'It is between three and four miles,' answered the lawyer.

'That's a long way for a person to live from his gate,' remarked his lordship.

Every few moments he saw something new to wonder at and admire. When he caught sight of the deer, some couched in the grass, some standing with their pretty antlered heads turned with a half-startled air towards the avenue as the carriage wheels disturbed them, he was enchanted.

'Has there been a circus,' he cried, 'or do they live here always? Whose are they?'

'They live here,' Mr Havisham told him. 'They belong to the Earl, your grandfather.'

It was not long after this that they saw the Castle. It rose up before them stately and beautiful and grey, the last rays of the sun casting dazzling lights on its many windows. It had turrets and battlements and towers; a great deal of ivy grew upon its walls; all the broad open space about it was laid out in terraces and lawns and beds of brilliant flowers.

'It's the most beautiful place I ever saw!' said Cedric, his round face flushing with pleasure. 'It reminds anyone of a king's palace. I saw a picture of one once in a fairy-book.'

He saw the great entrance door thrown open and many

servants standing in two lines looking at him. He wondered
why they were standing there, and admired their liveries very
much. He did not know that they were there to do honour to
the little boy to whom all this splendour would one day
belong—the beautiful Castle like the fairy king's palace, the
magnificent park, the grand old trees, the dells full of ferns
and bluebells where the hares and rabbits played, the dap-
pled, large-eyed deer couching in the deep grass. It was only
a couple of weeks since he had sat with Mr Hobbs among the
potatoes and canned peaches, with his legs dangling from the
high stool; it would not have been possible for him to realize
that he had very much to do with all this grandeur. At the
head of the line of servants there stood an elderly woman in a
rich, plain, black silk gown; she had grey hair and wore a
cap. As he entered the hall she stood nearer than the rest, and
the child thought from the look in her eyes that she was going
to speak to him. Mr Havisham, who held his hand, paused a
moment.

'This is Lord Fauntleroy, Mrs Mellon,' he said. 'Lord
Fauntleroy, this is Mrs Mellon, who is the housekeeper.'

Cedric gave her his hand, his eyes lighting up.

'Was it you who sent the cat?' he said. 'I'm much
obliged to you, ma'am.'

Mrs Mellon's handsome old face looked as pleased as
the face of the lodge-keeper's wife had done.

'I should know his lordship anywhere,' she said to Mr
Havisham. 'He has the Captain's face and way. It's a great
day, this, sir.'

Cedric wondered why it was a great day. He looked at
Mrs Mellon curiously. It seemed to him for a moment as if
there were tears in her eyes, and yet it was evident she was
not unhappy. She smiled down at him.

'The cat left two beautiful kittens here,' she said: 'they
shall be sent up to your lordship's nursery.'

Mr Havisham said a few words to her in a low voice.

'In the library, sir,' Mrs Mellon replied. 'His lordship is
to be taken there alone.'

* * *

A few minutes later the very tall footman in livery, who had escorted Cedric to the library door, opened it and announced: 'Lord Fauntleroy, my lord,' in quite a majestic tone. If he was only a footman, he felt it was rather a grand occasion when the heir came home to his own land and possessions, and was ushered into the presence of the old Earl, whose place and title he was to take.

Cedric crossed the threshold into the room. It was a very large and splendid room, with massive carven furniture in it, and shelves upon shelves of books; the furniture was so dark, and the draperies so heavy, the diamond-paned windows were so deep, and it seemed such a distance from one end of it to the other, that, since the sun had gone down, the effect of it all was rather gloomy. For a moment Cedric thought there was nobody in the room, but soon he saw that by the fire burning on the wide hearth there was a large easy chair, and that in that chair someone was sitting—someone who did not at first turn to look at him.

But he had attracted attention in one quarter at least. On the floor, by the armchair, lay a dog, a huge tawny mastiff with body and limbs almost as big as a lion's; and this great creature rose majestically and slowly, and marched towards the little fellow with a heavy step.

Then the person in the chair spoke. 'Dougal,' he called, 'come back, sir.'

But there was no more fear in little Lord Fauntleroy's heart than there was unkindness—he had been a brave little fellow all his life. He put his hand on the big dog's collar in the most natural way in the world, and they strayed forward together, Dougal sniffing as he went.

And then the Earl looked up. What Cedric saw was a large old man with shaggy white hair and eyebrows, and a nose like an eagle's beak between his deep fierce eyes. What the Earl saw was a graceful childish figure in a black velvet suit, with a lace collar, and with love-locks waving about the handsome, manly little face, whose eyes met his with a look of innocent good-fellowship. If the Castle was like the palace in a fairy story, it must be owned that little Lord Fauntleroy was himself rather like a small copy of the fairy prince, though he was not at all aware of the fact, and perhaps was rather a sturdy young model of a fairy. But there was a sudden glow of triumph and exultation in the fiery old Earl's heart as he saw what a strong beautiful boy this grandson was, and how unhesitatingly he looked up as he stood with his hand on the big dog's neck. It pleased the grim old nobleman that the child should show no shyness or fear, either of the dog or of himself.

Cedric looked at him just as he had looked at the woman at the lodge and at the housekeeper, and came quite close to him.

'Are you the Earl?' he said. 'I'm your grandson, you know, that Mr Havisham brought. I'm Lord Fauntleroy.'

He held out his hand because he thought it must be the polite and proper thing to do even with earls. 'I hope you are very well,' he continued, with the utmost friendliness. 'I'm very glad to see you.'

The Earl shook hands with him, with a curious gleam in his eyes; just at first he was so astonished that he scarcely knew what to say. He stared at the picturesque little apparition from under his shaggy brows, and took it all in from head to foot.

'Glad to see me, are you?' he said.

'Yes,' answered Lord Fauntleroy, 'very.'

There was a chair near him, and he sat down on it; it was a high-backed, rather tall chair, and his feet did not touch the floor when he had settled himself in it, but he seemed to be quite comfortable as he sat there and regarded his august relative intently and modestly.

'I've kept wondering what you would look like,' he remarked. 'I used to lie in my berth in the ship and wonder if you would be anything like my father.'

'Am I?' asked the Earl.

'Well,' Cedric replied, 'I was very young when he died,

and I may not remember exactly how he looked, but I don't think you are like him.'

'You are disappointed, I suppose?' suggested his grandfather.

'Oh no!' responded Cedric politely. 'Of course you would like anyone to look like your father; but of course you would enjoy the way your grandfather looked, even if he wasn't like your father. You know how it is yourself about admiring your relations.'

The Earl leaned back in his chair and stared. He could not be said to know how it was about admiring his relations. He had employed most of his noble leisure in quarrelling violently with them, in turning them out of his house, and applying abusive epithets to them; and they all hated him cordially.

'Any boy would love his grandfather,' continued Lord Fauntleroy, 'especially one that had been as kind to him as you have been.'

Another queer gleam came into the old nobleman's eyes.

'Oh,' he said, 'I have been kind to you, have I?'

'Yes,' answered Lord Fauntleroy brightly; 'I'm ever so much obliged to you about Bridget and the apple-woman and Dick!'

'Bridget!' exclaimed the Earl. 'Dick! The apple-woman!'

'Yes,' explained Cedric; 'the ones you gave me all that money for—the money you told Mr Havisham to give me if I wanted it.'

'Ha!' ejaculated his lordship. 'That's it, is it! The money you were to spend as you liked. What did you buy with it? I should like to hear something about that.'

He drew his shaggy eyebrows together and looked at the child sharply. He was secretly curious to know in what way the lad had indulged himself.

'Oh,' said Lord Fauntleroy, 'perhaps you didn't know about Dick and the apple-woman and Bridget. I forgot you lived such a long way off from them. They were particular friends of mine. And you see Michael had the fever—'

'Who's Michael?' asked the Earl.

'Michael is Bridget's husband, and they were in great
trouble. When a man is sick and can't work and has twelve
children you know how it is. And Michael had always been a
sober man. And Bridget used to come to our house and cry.
And the evening Mr Havisham was there, she was in the
kitchen crying because they had almost nothing to eat and
couldn't pay the rent; and I went in to see her, and Mr
Havisham sent for me and he said you had given him some
money for me. And I ran as fast as I could into the kitchen
and gave it to Bridget; and that made it all right; and Bridget
could scarcely believe her eyes. That's why I'm so obliged to
you.'

'Oh,' said the Earl in his deep voice, 'that was one of the
things you did for yourself, was it? What else?'

Dougal had been sitting by the tall chair; the great dog
had taken its place there when Cedric sat down. Several times
it had turned and looked up at the boy as if interested in the
conversation. Dougal was a solemn dog, who seemed to feel
altogether too big to take life's responsibilities lightly. The
old Earl, who knew the dog well, had watched it with secret
interest. Dougal was not a dog whose habit it was to make
acquaintances rashly, and the Earl wondered somewhat to see
how quietly the brute sat under the touch of the childish hand.
And, just at this moment, the big dog gave little Lord Fauntleroy one more look of dignified scrutiny, and deliberately
laid its huge, lion-like head on the boy's black-velvet knee.

The small hand went on stroking this new friend as
Cedric answered:

'Well, there was Dick,' he said. 'You'd like Dick, he's
so square.'

This was an Americanism the Earl was not prepared for.

'What does that mean?' he inquired.

Lord Fauntleroy paused a moment to reflect. He was not
very sure himself what it meant. He had taken it for granted
as meaning something very creditable because Dick had been
fond of using it.

'I think it means that he wouldn't cheat anyone,' he exclaimed, 'or hit a boy who was under his size, and that he blacks people's boots very well and makes them shine as much as he can. He's a professional boot-black.'

'And he's one of your acquaintances, is he?' said the Earl.

'He's an old friend of mine,' replied his grandson. 'Not quite as old as Mr Hobbs, but quite old. He gave me a present before the ship sailed.'

He put his hand into his pocket and drew forth a neatly folded red object and opened it with an air of affectionate pride. It was the red silk handkerchief with the large purple horseshoes and heads on it.

'He gave me this,' said his young lordship. 'I shall keep it always. You can wear it round your neck or keep it in your pocket. He bought it with the first money he earned after I bought Jake out and gave him the new brushes. It's a keepsake. I put some poetry in Mr Hobbs's watch. It was, "When this you see, remember me." When this I see I shall always remember Dick.'

The sensations of the Right Honourable the Earl of Dorincourt could scarcely be described. He was not an old nobleman who was very easily bewildered, because he had seen a great deal of the world; but here was something he found so novel that it almost took his lordly breath away, and caused him some singular emotions. He had never cared for children; he had been so occupied with his own pleasures that he had never had time to care for them. His own sons had not interested him when they were very young—though sometimes he remembered having thought Cedric's father a handsome and strong little fellow. He had been so selfish himself that he had missed the pleasure of seeing unselfishness in others, and he had not known how tender and faithful and affectionate a kind-hearted little child can be, and how innocent and unconscious are its simple, generous impulses. A boy had always seemed to him a most objectionable little animal, selfish and greedy and boisterous when not under strict restraint; his own two eldest sons had given their tutors constant trouble and annoyance, and of the younger one he fancied he had heard few complaints because the boy was of no particular importance. It had never once occurred to him that he should like his grandson; he had sent for the little Cedric because his pride impelled him to do so. If the boy was to take his place in the future, he did not wish his name to be ridiculous by descending to an uneducated boor. He had been convinced the boy would be a clownish fellow if he were brought up in America. He had no feeling of affection for the lad, his only hope was that he should find him decently well featured and with a respectable share of sense; he had been so disappointed in his other sons, and had been made so furious by Captain Errol's American marriage, that he had never once thought that anything creditable could come of it. When the footman had announced Lord Fauntleroy he had almost dreaded to look at the boy lest he should find him all he had feared. It was because of this feeling that he had ordered that the child should be sent to him alone. His pride could not endure that others should see his disappointment if he was to be disappointed. His proud, stubborn old heart therefore had leaped within him when the boy came forward with his graceful easy carriage, his fearless hand on the big dog's neck. Even in the moments when he had hoped the most, the Earl had never hoped that his grandson would look like that. It seemed almost too good to be true that this should be the boy he had dreaded to see—the child of the woman he so disliked—this little fellow with so much beauty and such a brave, childish grace! The Earl's stern composure was quite shaken by this startling surprise.

And then their talk began; and he was still more curiously moved and more and more puzzled. In the first place he was so used to seeing people rather afraid and embarrassed before him, that he had expected nothing else but that his grandson would be timid or shy. But Cedric was no more afraid of the Earl than he had been of Dougal. He was not bold; he was only innocently friendly, and he was not conscious that there should be any reason why he should be awkward or afraid. The Earl could not help seeing that the little boy took him for a friend and treated him as one, without having any doubt of him at all. It was quite plain as the little fellow sat there in his tall chair and talked in his friendly way that it had never occurred to him that this large, fierce-looking old man could be anything but kind to him, and rather pleased to see him there. And it was plain, too, that in his childish way he wished to please and interest his grandfather. Cross and hard-hearted and worldly as the old Earl was, he could not help feeling a secret and novel pleasure in this very confidence. After all, it was not disagreeable to meet someone who did not distrust or shrink from him, or seem to detect the ugly part of his nature; someone who looked at him with clear, unsuspecting eyes—if it was only a little boy in a black-velvet suit.

So the old man leaned back in his chair, and led his young companion on to telling him still more of himself, and with that odd gleam in his eyes watched the little fellow as he talked. Lord Fauntleroy was quite willing to answer all his questions and chatted on in his genial little way quite composedly. He told him all about Dick and Jerry and the apple-woman and Mr Hobbs; he described the Republican rally in all the glory of its banners and transparencies, torches and rockets. In the course of the conversation he reached the Fourth of July and the Revolution, and was just becoming enthusiastic, when he suddenly remembered something and stopped very abruptly.

'What is the matter?' demanded his grandfather. 'Why don't you go on?'

Lord Fauntleroy moved rather uneasily in his chair. It was evident to the Earl that Lord Fauntleroy was embarrassed by the thought which had just occurred to him.

'I was just thinking that perhaps you mightn't like it,' he replied. 'Perhaps someone belonging to you might have been there. I forgot you were an Englishman.'

'You can go on,' said my lord. 'No one belonging to me was there. You forgot you were an Englishman too.'

'Oh no,' said Cedric quickly. 'I'm an American!'

'You are an Englishman,' said the Earl grimly. 'Your father was an Englishman.'

It amused him a little to say this, but it did not amuse Cedric. The lad had never thought of such a development as this. He felt himself grow quite hot up to the roots of his hair.

'I was born in America,' he protested. 'You have to be an American if you are born in America. I beg your pardon,' with serious politeness and delicacy, 'for contradicting you. Mr Hobbs told me, if there was another war, you know, I should have to—to be an American!'

The Earl gave a grim half-laugh—it was short and grim, but it was a laugh.

'You would, would you?' he said.

He hated America and Americans, but it amused him to see how serious and interested this small patriot was. He thought that so good an American might make a rather good Englishman when he was a man.

They had not time to go very deep into the Revolution again—and indeed Lord Fauntleroy felt some delicacy about returning to the subject—before dinner was announced.

Cedric left his chair and went to his noble kinsman. He looked down at his gouty foot.

'Would you like me to help you?' he said politely. 'You could lean on me, you know. Once when Mr Hobbs hurt his foot with a potato barrel rolling on it, he used to lean on me.'

The big footman almost perilled his reputation and his situation by smiling. He was an aristocratic footman who had always lived in the best of noble families, and he had never smiled, indeed he would have felt himself a disgraced and vulgar footman if he had allowed himself to be led by any circumstance whatever into such an indiscretion as a smile. But he had a very narrow escape. He only just saved himself by staring straight over the Earl's head at a very ugly picture.

The Earl looked his valiant young relative over from head to foot.

'Do you think you could do it?' he asked gruffly.

'I *think* I could,' said Cedric. 'I'm strong. I'm seven, you know. You could lean on your stick on one side, and on me on the other. Dick says I've a good deal of muscle for a boy that's only seven.'

He shut his hand and moved it upwards to his shoulder, so that the Earl might see the muscle Dick had kindly approved of, and his face was so grave and earnest that the footman found it necessary to look very hard indeed at the ugly picture.

'Well,' said the Earl, 'you may try.'

Cedric gave him his stick, and began to assist him to rise. Usually the footman did this, and was violently sworn at when his lordship had an extra twinge of gout. The Earl was not a very polite person as a rule, and many a time the huge footmen about him quaked inside their imposing liveries.

But this evening he did not swear, though his gouty foot gave him more twinges than one. He chose to try an experiment. He got up slowly and put his hand on the small shoulder presented to him with so much courage. Little Lord Fauntleroy made a careful step forward, looking down at the gouty foot.

'Just lean on me,' he said with encouraging good cheer. 'I'll walk very slowly.'

If the Earl had been supported by the footman he would have rested less on his stick and more on his assistant's arm. And yet it was part of his experiment to let his grandson feel his burden as no light weight. It was quite a heavy weight indeed, and after a few steps his young lordship's face grew quite hot, and his heart beat rather fast, but he braced himself sturdily, remembering his muscle and Dick's approval of it.

'Don't be afraid of leaning on me,' he panted. 'I'm all right—if—if it isn't a very long way.'

It was not really very far to the dining-room, but it seemed rather a long way to Cedric before they reached the

chair at the head of the table. The hand on his shoulder
seemed to grow heavier at every step, and his face grew
redder and hotter, and his breath shorter, but he never thought
of giving up; he stiffened his childish muscles, held his head
erect and encouraged the Earl as he limped along.

'Does your foot hurt very much when you stand on it?'
he asked. 'Did you ever put it in hot water and mustard? Mr
Hobbs used to put his in hot water. Arnica is a very nice
thing, they tell me.'

The big dog stalked slowly beside them, and the big
footman followed; several times he looked very queer as he
watched the little figure making the very most of all its
strength, and bearing its burden with such goodwill. The
Earl too looked rather queer, once, as he glanced sideways
down at the flushed little face.

When they entered the room where they were to dine,
Cedric saw it was a very large and imposing one, and that the
footman who stood behind the chair at the head of the table
stared very hard as they came in.

But they reached the chair at last. The hand was removed from his shoulder and the Earl was fairly seated.

Cedric took out Dick's handkerchief and wiped his
forehead.

'It's a warm night, isn't it?' he said. 'Perhaps you need a
fire because—because of your foot, but it seems just a little
warm to me.'

His delicate consideration for his noble relative's feelings was such that he did not wish to seem to intimate that
any of his surroundings were unnecessary.

'You have been doing some rather hard work,' said the
Earl.

'Oh no!' said Lord Fauntleroy, 'it wasn't exactly hard,
but I got a little warm. A person will get warm in summer
time.'

And he rubbed his damp curls rather vigorously with the
gorgeous handkerchief. His own chair was placed at the other
end of the table, opposite his grandfather's. It was a chair

with arms, and intended for a much larger individual than himself; indeed everything he had seen so far—the great rooms, with their high ceilings, the massive furniture, the big footman, the big dog, the Earl himself—were all of proportions calculated to make this little lad feel that he was very small indeed. But that did not trouble him; he had never thought himself very large or important, and he was quite willing to accommodate himself even to circumstances which rather overpowered him.

Perhaps he had never looked so little a fellow as when seated now in his great chair, at the end of the table. Notwithstanding his solitary existence, the Earl chose to live in considerable state. He was fond of his dinner, and he dined in a formal style. Cedric looked at him across a glitter of splendid glass and plate, which to his unaccustomed eyes seemed quite dazzling. A stranger looking on might well have smiled at the picture—the great stately room, the big liveried servants, the bright lights, the glittering silver and glass, the fierce-looking old nobleman at the head of the table and the very small boy at the foot. Dinner was usually a very serious matter with the Earl—and it was a very serious matter with the cook, if his lordship was not pleased or had an indifferent appetite. Today, however, his appetite seemed a trifle better than usual, perhaps because he had something to think of besides the flavour of the *entrées* and the management of the gravies. His grandson gave him something to think of. He kept looking at him across the table. He did not say very much himself, but he managed to make the boy talk. He had never imagined that he could be entertained by hearing a child talk, but Lord Fauntleroy at once puzzled and amused him, and he kept remembering how he had let the childish shoulder feel his weight just for the sake of trying how far the boy's courage and endurance would go, and it pleased him to know that his grandson had not quailed and had not seemed to think even for a moment of giving up what he had undertaken to do.

'You don't wear your coronet all the time?' remarked Lord Fauntleroy respectfully.

'No,' replied the Earl with his grim smile; 'it is not becoming to me.'

'Mr Hobbs said you always wore it,' said Cedric; 'but after he thought it over, he said he supposed you must sometimes take it off to put your hat on.'

'Yes,' said the Earl, 'I take it off occasionally.'

And one of the footmen suddenly turned aside and gave a singular little cough behind his hand.

Cedric finished his dinner first, and then he leaned back in his chair and took a survey of the room.

'You must be very proud of your house,' he said, 'it's such a beautiful house. I never saw anything so beautiful; but of course as I'm only seven, I haven't seen much.'

'And you think I must be proud of it, do you?' said the Earl.

'I should think anyone would be proud of it,' replied Lord Fauntleroy. 'I should be proud of it if it were my house. Everything about it is beautiful. And the park, and those trees, how beautiful they are and how the leaves rustle!'

Then he paused an instant and looked across the table rather wistfully.

'It's a very big house for just two people to live in, isn't it?' he said.

'It is quite large enough for two,' answered the Earl. 'Do you find it too large?'

His little lordship hesitated a moment.

'I was only thinking,' he said, 'that if two people lived in it who were not very good companions, they might feel lonely sometimes.'

'Do you think I shall make a good companion?' inquired the Earl.

'Yes,' replied Cedric, 'I think you will. Mr Hobbs and I were great friends. He was the best friend I had except Dearest.'

The Earl made a quick movement of his bushy eyebrows.

'Who is Dearest?'

'She is my mother,' said Lord Fauntleroy in a rather low, quiet little voice.

Perhaps he was a trifle tired, as his bedtime was nearing, and perhaps after the excitement of the last few days it was natural he should be tired, so perhaps too the feeling of weariness brought to him a vague sense of loneliness in the remembrance that tonight he was not to sleep at home, watched over by the loving eyes of that 'best friend' of his. They had always been 'best friends', this boy and his young mother. He could not help thinking of her, and the more he thought of her the less he was inclined to talk, and by the time the dinner was at an end the Earl saw that there was a faint shadow on his face. But Cedric bore himself with excellent courage, and when they went back to the library, though the tall footman walked on one side of his master, the Earl's hand rested on his grandson's shoulder, though not so as before.

When the footman left them alone, Cedric sat down upon the hearthrug near Dougal. For a few minutes he stroked the dog's ears in silence and looked at the fire.

The Earl watched him. The boy's eyes looked wistful and thoughtful, and once or twice he gave a little sigh. The Earl sat still, and kept his eyes fixed on his grandson.

'Fauntleroy,' he said at last, 'what are you thinking of?'

Fauntleroy looked up with a manful effort at a smile.

'I was thinking about Dearest,' he said; 'and—and I think I'd better get up and walk up and down the room.'

He rose up, and put his hands in his small pockets, and began to walk to and fro. His eyes were very bright and his lips were pressed together, but he kept his head up and walked firmly. Dougal moved lazily and looked at him, and then stood up. He walked over to the child, and began to follow him uneasily. Fauntleroy drew one hand from his pocket and laid it on the dog's head.

'He's a very nice dog,' he said. 'He's my friend. He knows how I feel.'

'How do you feel?' asked the Earl.

It disturbed him to see the struggle the little fellow was having with his first feeling of homesickness, but it pleased him to see that he was making so brave an effort to bear it well. He liked this childish courage.

'Come here,' he said.

Fauntleroy went to him.

'I never was away from my own house before,' said the boy, with a troubled look in his brown eyes. 'It makes a person feel a strange feeling when he has to stay all night in another person's castle instead of in his own house. But Dearest is not very far away from me. She told me to remember that—and—and I'm seven—and I can look at the picture she gave me.'

He put his hand in his pocket, and brought out a small violet velvet-covered case.

'This is it,' he said. 'You see, you press this spring and it opens, and she is in there!'

He had come close to the Earl's chair, and, as he drew forth the little case, he leaned against the arm of it, and against the old man's arm too, as confidingly as if children had always leaned there.

'There she is,' he said, as the case opened; and he looked up with a smile.

The Earl knitted his brows; he did not wish to see the picture, but he looked at it in spite of himself; and there looked up at him from it such a pretty young face—a face so like the child's at his side—that it quite startled him.

'I suppose you think you are very fond of her?' he said.

'Yes,' answered Lord Fauntleroy, in a gentle tone, and with simple directness; 'I do think so, and I think it's true. You see Mr Hobbs was my friend, and Dick and Bridget and Mary and Michael, they were my friends too; but Dearest—well, she is my *close* friend, and we always tell each other everything. My father left her to me to take care of, and when I am a man I am going to work and earn money for her.'

'What do you think of doing?' inquired his grandfather.

His young lordship slipped down upon the hearthrug,

and sat there with the picture still in his hand. He seemed to be reflecting seriously before he answered.

'I did think perhaps I might go into business with Mr Hobbs,' he said; 'but I should *like* to be a president.'

'We'll send you to the House of Lords instead,' said his grandfather.

'Well,' remarked Lord Fauntleroy, 'if I *couldn't* be a president, and if that is a good business, I shouldn't mind. The grocery business is dull sometimes.'

Perhaps he was weighing the matter in his mind, for he sat very quiet after this, and looked at the fire for some time.

The Earl did not speak again. He leaned back in his chair and watched him. A great many strange new thoughts passed through the old nobleman's mind. Dougal had stretched himself out and gone to sleep with his head on his huge paws. There was a long silence.

In about half an hour's time Mr Havisham was ushered in. The great room was very still when he entered. The Earl was still leaning back in his chair. He moved as Mr Havisham approached and held up his hand in a gesture of warning—it seemed as if he had scarcely intended to make the gesture—as if it were almost involuntary. Dougal was still asleep, and close beside the great dog, sleeping also, with his curly head upon his arm, lay little Lord Fauntleroy.

SIX

The Earl and His Grandson

When Lord Fauntleroy wakened in the morning—he had not wakened at all when he had been carried to bed the night before—the first sounds he was conscious of were the crackling of a wood fire and the murmur of voices.

'You will be careful, Dawson, not to say anything about it,' he heard someone say. 'He does not know why she is not to be with him, and the reason is to be kept from him.'

'If them's his lordship's orders, mem,' another voice answered, 'they'll have to be kep', I suppose. But, if you'll excuse the liberty, mem, as it's between ourselves, servant or no servant, all I have to say is, it's a cruel thing—parting that poor, pretty, young widdered cre'tur from her own flesh and blood, and him such a little beauty and a nobleman born. James and Thomas, mem, last night in the servants' hall, they both of 'em say as they never see anythink in their two lives—nor yet no other gentleman in livery—like that little fellow's ways, as innercent an' polite an' interested as if he'd been sitting there dining with his best friend—and the temper of a' angel, instead of one (if you'll excuse me, mem), as it's well known is enough to curdle your blood in your veins at times. And as to looks, mem, when we was rung for, James and me, to go into the library and bring him upstairs, and James lifted him up in his arms, what with his little innercent face all red and rosy, and his little head on James's shoulder and his hair hanging down, all curly an' shinin', a prettier, takiner sight you'd never wish to see. An' it's my opinion, my lord wasn't to it neither, for he looked at him, and he says to James, "See you don't wake him!" he says.'

Cedric moved on his pillow, and turned over, opening his eyes.

There were two women in the room. Everything was bright and cheerful with gay-flowered chintz. There was a fire on the hearth, and the sunshine was streaming in through the ivy-entwined windows. Both women came towards him, and he saw that one of them was Mrs Mellon, the housekeeper, and the other a comfortable, middle-aged woman, with a face as kind and good-humored as a face could be.

'Good morning, my lord,' said Mrs Mellon. 'Did you sleep well?'

His lordship rubbed his eyes and smiled.

'Good morning,' he said. 'I didn't know I was here.'

'You were carried upstairs when you were asleep,' said the housekeeper. 'This is your bedroom, and this is Dawson, who is to take care of you.'

Fauntleroy sat up in bed and held out his hand to Dawson as he had held it out to the Earl.

'How do you do, ma'am?' he said. 'I'm much obliged to you for coming to take care of me.'

'You can call her Dawson, my lord,' said the housekeeper with a smile. 'She is used to being called Dawson.'

'*Miss* Dawson or *Mrs* Dawson?' inquired his lordship.

'Just Dawson, my lord,' said Dawson herself, beaming all over. 'Neither Miss nor Missis, bless your little heart! Will you get up now, and let Dawson dress you, and then have your breakfast in the nursery?'

'I learned to dress myself many years ago, thank you,' answered Fauntleroy. 'Dearest taught me. "Dearest" is my mamma. We had only Mary to do all the work—washing and all—and so of course it wouldn't do to give her so much trouble. I can take my bath, too, pretty well, if you'll just be kind enough to 'zamine the corners after I'm done.'

Dawson and the housekeeper exchanged glances.

'Dawson will do anything you ask her to,' said Mrs Mellon.

'That I will, bless him,' said Dawson, in her comforting, good-humoured voice. 'He shall dress himself if he likes, and I'll stand by, ready to help him if he wants me.'

'Thank you,' responded Lord Fauntleroy; 'it's a little hard sometimes about the buttons, you know, and then I have to ask somebody.'

He thought Dawson a very kind woman, and before the bath and the dressing were finished they were excellent friends, and he had found out a great deal about her. He had discovered that her husband had been a soldier and had been killed in a real battle, and that her son was a sailor, and was away on a long cruise, and that he had seen pirates and cannibals and Chinese people and Turks, and that he brought home strange shells, and pieces of coral which Dawson was ready to show at any moment, some of them being in her trunk. All this was very interesting. He also found out that she had taken care of little children all her life, and that she had just come from a great house in another part of England, where she had been taking care of a beautiful little girl whose name was Lady Gwyneth Vaughan.

'And she is a sort of relation of your lordship's,' said Dawson. 'And perhaps some time you may see her.'

'Do you think I shall?' said Fauntleroy. 'I should like that. I never knew any little girls, but I always like to look at them.'

When he went into the adjoining room to take his breakfast and saw what a great room it was, and found there was another adjoining it, which Dawson told him was his also, the feeling that he was very small indeed came over him again so strongly that he confided it to Dawson, as he sat down to the table on which the pretty breakfast service was arranged.

'I am a very little boy,' he said rather wistfully, 'to live in such a large castle, and have so many big rooms—don't you think so?'

'Oh, come,' said Dawson, 'you feel just a little strange at first, that's all; but you'll get over that very soon, and then you'll like it here. It's such a beautiful place, you know.'

'It's a very beautiful place of course,' said Fauntleroy with a little sigh, 'but I should like it better if I didn't miss Dearest so. I always had my breakfast with her in the morning, and put the sugar and cream in her tea for her, and handed her the toast. That made it very sociable of course.'

'Oh well,' answered Dawson comfortably, 'you know you can see her every day, and there's no knowing how much you'll have to tell her. Bless you, wait till you've walked about a bit and seen things—the dogs, and the stables with all the horses in them. There's one of them I know you'll like to see—'

'Is there?' exclaimed Fauntleroy. 'I'm very fond of horses. I was very fond of Jim. He was the horse that belonged to Mr Hobbs's grocery wagon. He was a beautiful horse when he wasn't balky.'

'Well,' said Dawson, 'you just wait till you've seen what's in the stables. And, deary me, you haven't looked even into the very next room yet!'

'What is there?' asked Fauntleroy.

'Wait until you've had your breakfast, and then you shall see,' said Dawson.

At this he naturally began to grow curious, and he applied himself assiduously to his breakfast. It seemed to him that there must be something worth looking at in the next room; Dawson had such a consequential, mysterious air.

'Now then,' he said, slipping off his seat a few minutes later; 'I've had enough. Can I go and look at it?'

Dawson nodded and led the way, looking more mysterious and important than ever. He began to be very much interested indeed.

When she opened the door of the room, he stood upon the threshold and looked about him in amazement. He did not speak; he only put his hands in his pockets and stood there flushing up to his forehead and looking in.

He flushed up because he was so surprised and, for the moment, excited. To see such a place was enough to surprise any ordinary boy.

The room was a large one too, as all the rooms seemed to be, and it appeared to him more beautiful than the rest, only in a different way. The furniture was not so massive and antique as was that in the rooms he had seen downstairs; the draperies and rugs and walls were brighter; there were shelves full of books, and on the tables were numbers of toys— beautiful, ingenious things—such as he had looked at with wonder and delight through the shop windows in New York.

'It looks like a boy's room,' he said at last, catching his breath a little. 'Who do they belong to?'

'Go and look at them,' said Dawson. 'They belong to you!'

'To me!' he cried. 'To me! Why do they belong to me? Who gave them to me?' And he sprang forward with a gay little shout. It seemed almost too much to be believed. 'It was Grandpapa!' he said, with his eyes as bright as stars. 'I know it was Grandpapa!'

'Yes, it was his lordship,' said Dawson; 'and if you will be a nice little gentleman, and not fret about things, and will enjoy yourself, and be happy all the day, he will give you anything you ask for.'

It was a tremendously exciting morning. There were so many things to be examined, so many experiments to be tried; each novelty was so absorbing that he could scarcely turn from it to look at the next. And it was so curious to know that all this had been prepared for himself alone; that, even before he had left New York, people had come down from London to arrange the rooms he was to occupy, and had provided the books and playthings most likely to interest him.

'Did you ever know anyone,' he said to Dawson, 'who had such a kind grandfather?'

Dawson's face wore an uncertain expression for a moment. She had not a very high opinion of his lordship the Earl. She had not been in the house many days, but she had been there long enough to hear the old nobleman's peculiarities discussed very freely in the servants' hall.

'An' of all the wicious, savage, hill-tempered hold fellows it was ever my hill-luck to wear livery hunder,' the tallest footman had said, 'he's the wiolentest and wust by a long shot.'

And this particular footman, whose name was Thomas, had also repeated to his companions below stairs some of the Earl's remarks to Mr Havisham, when they had been discussing these very preparations.

'Give him his own way and fill his rooms with toys,' my lord had said. 'Give him what will amuse him, and he'll forget about his mother quickly enough. Amuse him, and fill his mind with other things, and we shall have no trouble. That's boy nature.'

So perhaps, having had this truly amiable object in view, it did not please him so very much to find it did not seem to be exactly this particular boy's nature. The Earl had passed a bad night and had spent the morning in his room; but at noon, after he had lunched, he sent for his grandson.

Fauntleroy answered the summons at once. He came down the broad staircase with a bounding step; the Earl heard him run across the hall, and then the door opened and he came in with red cheeks and sparkling eyes.

'I was waiting for you to send for me,' he said. 'I was ready a long time ago. I'm *ever* so much obliged to you for all those things! I'm *ever* so much obliged to you! I have been playing with them all morning.'

'Oh,' said the Earl, 'you like them, do you?'

'I like them so much—well, I couldn't tell you how much!' said Fauntleroy, his face glowing with delight. 'There's one that's like baseball, only you play it on a board with black and white pegs, and you keep your score with some counters on a wire. I tried to teach Dawson, but she couldn't quite understand it just at first—you see she never played baseball, being a lady; and I'm afraid I wasn't very good at explaining it to her. But you know all about it, don't you?'

'I'm afraid I don't,' replied the Earl. 'It's an American game, isn't it? Is it something like cricket?'

'I never saw cricket,' said Fauntleroy; 'but Mr Hobbs took me several times to see baseball. It's a splendid game. You get so excited! Would you like me to go and get my game and show it to you? Perhaps it would amuse you and make you forget about your foot. Does your foot hurt you very much this morning?'

'More than I enjoy,' was the answer.

'Then perhaps you couldn't forget it,' said the little fellow anxiously. 'Perhaps it would bother you to be told about the game. Do you think it would amuse you, or do you think it would bother you?'

'Go and get it,' said the Earl.

It certainly was a novel entertainment this—making a companion of a child who offered to teach him to play games, but the very novelty of it amused him. There was a smile lurking about the Earl's mouth when Cedric came back with the box containing the game in his arms, and an expression of the most eager interest on his face.

'May I pull that little table over here to your chair?' he asked.

'Ring for Thomas,' said the Earl. 'He will place it for you.'

'Oh, I can do it myself,' answered Fauntleroy. 'It's not very heavy.'

'Very well,' replied his grandfather. The lurking smile deepened on the old man's face as he watched the little fellow's preparations; there was such an absorbed interest in them. The small table was dragged forward and placed by his chair, and the game taken from its box and arranged upon it.

'It's very interesting when you once begin,' said Fauntleroy. 'You see, the black pegs can be your side and the white ones mine. They're men, you know, and once round the field is a home run and counts one—and these are the outs—and here is the first base and that's the second and that's the third and that's the home-base.'

He entered into the details of explanation with the greatest animation. He showed all the attitudes of pitcher and catcher and batter in the real game, and gave a dramatic description of a wonderful 'hot ball' he had seen caught on the glorious occasion on which he had witnessed a match in company with Mr Hobbs. His vigorous, graceful little body, his eager gestures, his simple enjoyment of it all were pleasant to behold.

When at last the explanations and illustrations were at an end and the game began in good earnest, the Earl still found himself entertained. His young companion was wholly absorbed; he played with all his childish heart; his gay little laughs when he made a good throw, his enthusiasm over a 'home run', his impartial delight over his own good luck or his opponent's, would have given a flavour to any game.

If a week before anyone had told the Earl of Dorincourt that on that particular morning he would be forgetting his gout and his bad temper in a child's game, played with black and white wooden pegs, on a gaily painted board, with a curly-headed small boy for a companion, he would without doubt have made himself very unpleasant; and yet he certainly had forgotten himself when the door opened and Thomas announced a visitor.

The visitor in question, who was an elderly gentleman in black, and no less a person than the clergyman of the parish, was so startled by the amazing scene which met his eye that he almost fell back a pace, and ran some risk of colliding with Thomas.

There was in fact no part of his duty that the Reverend Mr Mordaunt found so decidedly unpleasant as that part which compelled him to call upon his noble patron at the Castle. His noble patron indeed usually made these visits as disagreeable as it lay in his lordly power to make them. He abhorred churches and charities, and flew into violent rages when any of his tenantry took the liberty of being poor and ill and needed assistance. When his gout was at its worst, he did not hesitate to announce that he would not be bored and irritated by being told stories of their miserable fortunes; when his gout troubled him less and he was in a somewhat more humane frame of mind, he would perhaps give the rector some money, after having bullied him in the most painful manner, and berated the whole parish for its shiftlessness and imbecility. But, whatsoever his mood, he never failed to make as many sarcastic and embarrassing speeches as possible, and to cause the Reverend Mr Mordaunt to wish it were proper and Christian-like to throw something heavy at him. During all the years in which Mr Mordaunt had been in charge of Dorincourt parish, the rector certainly did not remember having seen his lordship, of his own free will, do anyone a kindness, or, under any circumstances whatever, show that he thought of anyone but himself.

He had called today to speak to him of a specially pressing case, and as he had walked up the avenue, he had, for two reasons, dreaded his visit more than usual. In the first place, he knew that his lordship had for several days been suffering from the gout, and had been in so villainous a humour that rumours of it had even reached the village—carried there by one of the young women servants to her sister, who kept a little shop and retailed darning-needles and cotton and peppermints and gossip, as a means of earning an honest living. What Mrs Dibble did not know about the Castle and its inmates, and the farmhouses and their inmates, and the village and its population, was really not worth being talked about. And of course she knew everything about the Castle, because her sister Jane Shorts was one of the upper housemaids, and was very friendly and intimate with Thomas.

'And the way his lordship do go on!' said Mrs Dibble, over the counter, 'and the way he do use language, Mr Thomas told Jane herself, no flesh or blood as in livery could stand—for throw a plate of toast at Mr Thomas hisself, he did, not more than two days since, and if it weren't for other things being agreeable and the society below stairs most genteel, warning would have been gave within a' hour!'

And the rector heard all this, for somehow the Earl was a favourite black sheep in the cottages and farmhouses, and his bad behaviour gave many a good woman something to talk about when she had company to tea.

And the second reason was even worse, because it was a new one and had been talked about with the most excited interest.

Who did not know of the old nobleman's fury when his handsome son the Captain had married the American lady? Who did not know how cruelly he had treated the Captain, and how the big, gay, sweet-smiling young man, who was the only member of the grand family anyone liked, had died in a foreign land, poor and unforgiven? Who did not know how fiercely his lordship had hated the poor young creature who had been this son's wife, and how he had hated the thought of her child and never meant to see the boy—until his two sons died and left him without an heir? And then, who did not know that he had looked forward without any affection or pleasure to his grandson's coming, and that he had made up his mind that he should find the boy a vulgar, awkward, pert American lad, more likely to disgrace his noble name than to honour it?

The proud, angry old man thought he had kept all his thoughts secret. He did not suppose anyone had dared to guess at, even less talk over what he felt, and dreaded; but his servants watched him, and read his face and his ill-humours and fits of gloom, and discussed them in the servants' hall. And while he thought himself quite secure from the common herd, Thomas was telling Jane and the cook and the butler and the housemaids and the other footmen that it was his opinion that 'the hold man was wuss than usual a-thinkin' hover the Captin's boy, an' hanticipatin' as he won't be no credit to the fambly. An' serve him right,' added Thomas; 'hit's 'is hown fault. Wot can he iggspect from a child brought up in pore circumstances in that there low Hamerica?'

And as the Reverend Mr Mordaunt walked under the great trees he remembered that this questionable little boy had arrived at the Castle only the evening before, and that there were nine chances to one that his lordship's worst fears were realized, and twenty-two chances to one that if the poor little fellow had disappointed him, the Earl was even now in a tearing rage, and ready to vent all his rancour on the first person who called—which it appeared probable would be his reverend self.

Judge then of his amazement when, as Thomas opened the library door, his ears were greeted by a delightful ring of childish laughter.

'That's two out!' almost shouted an excited, clear little voice. 'You see it's two out!'

And there was the Earl's chair, and the gout-stool, and his foot on it; and by him a small table and a game on it; and quite close to him, actually leaning against his arm and his ungouty knee, was a little boy with face glowing, and eyes dancing with excitement. 'It's two out!' the little stranger cried. 'You hadn't any luck that time, had you?' And then they both recognized at once that someone had come in.

The Earl glanced around, knitted his shaggy eyebrows as he had a trick of doing, and when he saw who it was, Mr Mordaunt was still more surprised to see that he looked even less disagreeable than usual instead of more so. In fact, he looked almost as if he had forgotten for the moment how disagreeable he was, and how unpleasant he really could make himself when he tried.

'Ah,' he said in his harsh voice, but giving his hand rather graciously, 'good morning, Mordaunt. I've found a new employment, you see.'

He put his other hand on Cedric's shoulder—perhaps deep down in his heart there was a stir of gratified pride that it was such an heir he had to present; there was a spark of something like pleasure in his eyes as he moved the boy slightly forward.

'This is the new Lord Fauntleroy,' he said. 'Fauntleroy, this is Mr Mordaunt, the rector of the parish.'

Fauntleroy looked up at the gentleman in the clerical garments, and gave him his hand.

'I am very glad to make your acquaintance, sir,' he said, remembering the words he had heard Mr Hobbs use on one or two occasions when he had been greeting a new customer with ceremony. Cedric felt quite sure that one ought to be more than usually polite to a minister.

Mr Mordaunt held the small hand in his a moment as he looked down at the child's face, smiling involuntarily. He liked the little fellow from that instant—as in fact people always did like him. And it was not the boy's beauty and grace which most appealed to him; it was the simple, natural kindliness in the little lad which made any words he uttered, however quaint and unexpected, sound pleasant and sincere. As the rector looked at Cedric, he forgot to think of the Earl at all. Nothing in the world is so strong as a kind heart, and somehow this kind little heart, though it was only the heart of a child, seemed to clear all the atmosphere of the big gloomy room and make it brighter.

'I am delighted to make your acquaintance, Lord Fauntleroy,' said the rector. 'You made a long journey to come to us. A great many people will be glad to know you made it safely.'

'It *was* a long way,' answered Fauntleroy; 'but Dearest, my mother, was with me, and I wasn't lonely. Of course you are never lonely if your mother is with you; and the ship was beautiful.'

'Take a chair, Mordaunt,' said the Earl. Mr Mordaunt sat down. He glanced from Fauntleroy to the Earl.

'Your lordship is greatly to be congratulated,' he said warmly. But the Earl plainly had no intention of showing his feelings on the subject.

'He is like his father,' he said rather gruffly. 'Let us hope he'll conduct himself more creditably.' And then he added, 'well, what is it this morning, Mordaunt? Who is in trouble now?'

This was not as bad as Mr Mordaunt had expected, but he hesitated a second before he began.

'It is Higgins,' he said; 'Higgins of Edge Farm. He has been very unfortunate. He was ill himself last autumn, and his children had scarlet fever. I can't say that he is a very good manager, but he has had ill-luck, and of course he is behindhand in many ways. He is in trouble about his rent now. Newick tells him if he doesn't pay it he must leave the place; and of course that would be a very serious matter. His wife is ill, and he came to me yesterday to beg me to see you about it, and ask you for time. He thinks if you would give him time he could catch up again.'

'They all think that,' said the Earl, looking rather black.

Fauntleroy made a movement forward. He had been standing between his grandfather and the visitor, listening with all his might. He had begun to be interested in Higgins at once. He wondered how many children there were, and if the scarlet fever had hurt them very much. His eyes were wide open and were fixed upon Mr Mordaunt with intense interest as that gentleman went on with the conversation.

'Higgins is a well-meaning man,' said the rector, making an effort to strengthen his plea.

'He is a bad enough tenant,' replied his lordship. 'And he is always behindhand, Newick tells me.'

'He is in great trouble now,' said the rector. 'He is very fond of his wife and children, and if the farm is taken from him they may literally starve. He cannot give them the nourishing things they need. Two of the children were left very low after the fever, and the doctor orders for them wine and luxuries that Higgins cannot afford.'

At this Fauntleroy moved a step nearer.

'That was the way with Michael,' he said.

The Earl slightly started. 'I forgot *you*!' he said, 'I forgot we had a philanthropist in the room. Who was Michael?' And the gleam of queer amusement came back into the old man's deep-set eyes.

'He was Bridget's husband, who had the fever,' answered Fauntleroy; 'and he couldn't pay the rent or buy wine and things. And you gave me that money to help him.'

The Earl drew his brows together into a curious frown, which somehow was scarcely grim at all. He glanced across at Mr Mordaunt.

'I don't know what sort of a landed proprietor he will make,' he said. 'I told Havisham the boy was to have what he wanted—and what he wanted, it seems, was money to give to beggars.'

'Oh, but they weren't beggars,' said Fauntleroy eagerly. 'Michael was a splendid bricklayer! They all worked.'

'Oh,' said the Earl, 'they were not beggars. They were splendid bricklayers and boot-blacks and apple-women.'

He bent his gaze on the boy for a few seconds in silence. The fact was that a new thought was coming to him, and though perhaps it was not promoted by the noblest emotions, it was not a bad thought. 'Come here,' he said at last.

Fauntleroy went and stood as near to him as possible without encroaching on the gouty foot.

'What would *you* do in this case?' his lordship asked.

It must be confessed that Mr Mordaunt experienced for the moment a curious sensation. Being a man of great thoughtfulness, and having spent so many years on the estate of Dorincourt, knowing the tenantry, rich and poor, the people of the village, honest and industrious, dishonest and lazy, he realized very strongly what power for good or evil would be given in the future to this one small boy standing there, his brown eyes wide open, his hands deep in his pockets; and the thought came to him also that a great deal of power might perhaps, through the caprice of a proud, self-indulgent old man, be given to him now, and that if his young nature were not a simple and generous one, it might be the worst thing that could happen, not only for others, but for himself.

'And what would *you* do in such a case?' demanded the Earl.

Fauntleroy drew a little nearer, and laid one hand on his knee, with the most confiding air of good comradeship.

'If I were very rich,' he said, 'and not only just a little boy, I should let him stay, and give him the things for his children; but then, I am only a boy.' Then, after a second's pause, in which his face brightened visibly: '*You* can do anything, can't you?' he said.

'Humph!' said my lord, staring at him. 'That's your opinion, is it?' And he was not displeased either.

'I mean you can give anyone anything,' said Fauntleroy. 'Who's Newick?'

'He is my agent,' answered the Earl, 'and some of my tenants are not overfond of him.'

'Are you going to write him a letter now?' inquired Fauntleroy. 'Shall I bring you the pen and ink? I can take the game off this table.'

It plainly had not for an instant occurred to him that Newick would be allowed to do his worst.

The Earl paused a moment, still looking at him. 'Can you write?' he asked.

'Yes,' answered Cedric, 'but not very well.'

'Move the things from the table,' commanded my lord, 'and bring the pen and ink, and a sheet of paper from my desk.'

Mr Mordaunt's interest began to increase. Fauntleroy did as he was told very deftly. In a few moments the sheet of paper, the big inkstand and the pen were ready.

'There,' he said gaily, 'now you can write it.'

'You are to write it,' said the Earl.

'I!' exclaimed Fauntleroy, and a flush overspread his forehead. 'Will it do if I write it? I don't always spell quite right when I haven't a dictionary and nobody tells me.'

'It will do,' answered the Earl. 'Higgins will not complain of the spelling. I'm not the philanthropist; you are. Dip your pen in the ink.'

Fauntleroy took up the pen and dipped it in the ink-bottle, then he arranged himself in position, leaning on the table.

'Now,' he inquired, 'what must I say?'

'You may say, "Higgins is not to be interfered with for the present", and sign it "Fauntleroy",' said the Earl.

Fauntleroy dipped his pen in the ink again, and, resting his arm, began to write. It was rather a slow and serious process, but he gave his whole soul to it. After a while, however, the manuscript was complete, and he handed it to his grandfather with a smile slightly tinged with anxiety.

'Do you think it will do?' he asked.

The Earl looked at it, and the corners of his mouth twitched a little.

'Yes,' he answered; 'Higgins will find it entirely satisfactory.' And he handed it to Mr Mordaunt.

What Mr Mordaunt found written was this:

> Dear mr Newik if you pleas mr higins is not to be inturfeared with for the present and oblige
>
> Yours rispecferly
> FAUNTLEROY

'Mr Hobbs always signed his letters that way,' said Fauntleroy; 'and I thought I'd better say "please". Is that exactly the right way to spell "interfered"?'

'It's not exactly the way it is spelled in the dictionary,' answered the Earl.

'I was afraid of that,' said Fauntleroy. 'I ought to have asked. You see that's the way with words of more than one syllable; you have to look in the dictionary. It's always safest. I'll write it over again.'

And write it over again he did, making quite an imposing copy, and taking precautions in the matter of spelling by consulting the Earl himself.

'Spelling is a curious thing,' he said. 'It's so often different from what you expect it to be. I used to think ''please'' was spelled p-l-e-e-s, but it isn't, you know; and you'd think ''dear'' was spelled d-e-r-e, if you didn't inquire. Sometimes it almost discourages you.'

When Mr Mordaunt went away he took the letter with him, and he took something else with him also—namely, a pleasanter feeling and a more hopeful one than he had ever carried home with him down that avenue on any previous visit he had made at Dorincourt Castle.

When he was gone Fauntleroy, who had accompanied him to the door, went back to his grandfather.

'May I go to Dearest now?' he said. 'I think she will be waiting for me.'

The Earl was silent for a moment.

'There is something in the stable for you to see first,' he said. 'Ring the bell.'

'If you please,' said Fauntleroy, with his quick little flush, 'I'm very much obliged; but I think I'd better see it tomorrow. She will be expecting me all the time.'

'Very well,' answered the Earl. 'We will order the carriage.' Then he added dryly: 'It's a pony.'

Fauntleroy drew a long breath.

'A pony!' he exclaimed. 'Whose pony is it?'

'Yours,' replied the Earl.

'Mine?' cried the little fellow. 'Mine—like the things upstairs?'

'Yes,' said his grandfather. 'Would you like to see it? Shall I order it to be brought round?'

Fauntleroy's cheeks grew redder and redder.

'I never thought I should have a pony!' he said. 'I never thought that! How glad Dearest will be. You give me *everything*, don't you?'

'Do you wish to see it?' inquired the Earl.

Fauntleroy drew a long breath. 'I *want* to see it,' he said. 'I want to see it so much I can hardly wait. But I'm afraid there isn't time.'

'You *must* go and see your mother this afternoon?' asked the Earl. 'You think you can't put it off?'

'Why,' said Fauntleroy, 'she has been thinking about me all the morning, and I have been thinking about her.'

'Oh,' said the Earl, 'you have, have you? Ring the bell.'

As they drove down the avenue, under the arching trees, he was rather silent. But Fauntleroy was not. He talked about the pony. What colour was it? How big was it? What was its name? What did it like to eat best? How old was it? How early in the morning might he get up and see it?

'Dearest will be so glad!' he kept saying. 'She will be so much obliged to you for being so kind to me! She knows I always liked ponies so much, but we never thought I should have one. There was a little boy on Fifth Avenue who had one, and he used to ride out every morning and we used to take a walk past his house to see him.'

He leaned back against the cushions and regarded the Earl with rapt interest for a few minutes and in entire silence.

'I think you must be the best person in the world,' he burst forth at last. 'You are always doing good, aren't you? —and thinking about other people. Dearest says that is the best kind of goodness; not to think about yourself, but to think about other people. That is just the way you are, isn't it?'

His lordship was so dumbfounded to find himself presented in such agreeable colours that he did not know exactly what to say. He felt that he needed time for reflection. To see each of his ugly, selfish motives changed into a good and generous one by the simplicity of a child was a singular experience.

Fauntleroy went on, still regarding him with admiring eyes—those great, clear, innocent eyes!

'You make so many people happy,' he said. 'There's Michael and Bridget and their twelve children, and the apple-woman and Dick and Mr Hobbs, and Mr Higgins and Mrs Higgins and their children, and Mr Mordaunt—because of course he was glad—and Dearest and me, about the pony and all the other things. Do you know, I've counted it up on my fingers and in my mind, and it's twenty-seven people you've been kind to. That's a good many—twenty-seven!'

'And I was the person who was kind to them, was I?' said the Earl.

'Why, yes, you know,' answered Fauntleroy. 'You made them all happy. Do you know,' with some delicate hesitation, 'that people are sometimes mistaken about earls when they don't know them. Mr Hobbs was. I am going to write to him and tell him about it.'

'What was Mr Hobbs's opinion of earls?' asked his lordship.

'Well, you see, the difficulty was,' replied his young companion, 'that he didn't know any, and he'd only read about them in books. He thought—you mustn't mind it—that they were gory tyrants; and he said he wouldn't have them hanging around his store. But if he'd known *you,* I'm sure he would have felt quite different. I shall tell him about you.'

'What shall you tell him?'

'I shall tell him,' said Fauntleroy, glowing with enthusiasm, 'that you are the kindest man I ever heard of. And you are always thinking of other people, and making them happy, and—and I hope when I grow up I shall be just like you.'

'Just like me!' repeated his lordship, looking at the little kindling face. And a dull red crept up under his withered skin, and he suddenly turned his eyes away and looked out of the carriage window at the great beech trees, with the sun shining on their glossy, red-brown leaves.

'*Just* like you,' said Fauntleroy, adding modestly: 'If I can. Perhaps I'm not good enough, but I'm going to try.'

The carriage rolled on down the stately avenue under the beautiful, broad-branched trees, through the spaces of green shade and lanes of golden sunlight. Fauntleroy saw again the lovely places where the ferns grew high and the bluebells swayed in the breeze; he saw the deer, standing or lying in the deep grass, turn their large startled eyes as the carriage passed, and caught glimpses of the brown rabbits as they scurried away. He heard the whir of the partridges and the calls and songs of the birds, and it all seemed even more beautiful to him than before. All his heart was filled with pleasure and happiness in the beauty that was on every side. But the old Earl saw and heard very different things, though he was apparently looking out too. He saw a long life, in which there had been neither generous deeds nor kind thoughts; he saw years in which a man who had been young and strong and rich and powerful had used his youth and strength and wealth and power only to please himself and kill time as the days and years succeeded each other; he saw this man, when the time had been killed and old age had come, solitary and without real friends in the midst of all his splendid wealth; he saw people who disliked or feared him, and people who would flatter and cringe to him, but no one who really cared whether he lived or died, unless they had something to gain or lose by it. He looked out on the broad acres which belonged to him, and he knew what Fauntleroy did not—how far they extended, what wealth they represented and how many people had homes on their soil. And he knew too—another thing Fauntleroy did not—that in all those homes, humble or well to do, there was probably not one person, however much he envied the wealth and stately name and power, and however willing he would have been to possess them, who would for an instant have thought of calling the noble owner 'good', or wishing, as this simple-souled little boy had, to be like him.

And it was not exactly pleasant to reflect upon, even for a cynical, worldly old man, who had been sufficient unto himself for seventy years and who had never deigned to care what opinion the world held of him so long as it did not interfere with his comfort or entertainment. And the fact was, indeed, that he had never before condescended to reflect upon it at all, and he only did so now because a child had believed him better than he was and by wishing to follow in his illustrious footsteps and imitate his example, had suggested to him the curious question whether he was exactly the person to take as a model.

Fauntleroy thought the Earl's foot must be hurting him, his brows knitted themselves together so, as he looked out at the park; and thinking this, the considerate little fellow tried not to disturb him, and enjoyed the trees and the ferns and the deer in silence. But at last the carriage, having passed the gates and bowled through the green lanes for a short distance, stopped. They had reached Court Lodge; and Fauntleroy was out upon the ground almost before the big footman had time to open the carriage door.

The Earl wakened from his reverie with a start.

'What!' he said. 'Are we here?'

'Yes,' said Fauntleroy. 'Let me give you your stick. Just lean on me when you get out.'

'I am not going to get out,' replied his lordship brusquely.

'Not—not to see Dearest?' exclaimed Fauntleroy with astonished face.

' "Dearest" will excuse me,' said the Earl dryly. 'Go to her and tell her that not even a new pony would keep you away.'

'She will be disappointed,' said Fauntleroy. 'She will want to see you very much.'

'I am afraid not,' was the answer. 'The carriage will call for you as we come back. Tell Jefferies to drive on, Thomas.'

Thomas closed the carriage door: and, after a puzzled look, Fauntleroy ran up the drive. The Earl had the opportunity— as Mr Havisham once had—of seeing a pair of handsome, strong little legs flash over the ground with astonishing rapidity. Evidently their owner had no intention of losing any time. The carriage rolled slowly away, but his lordship did not at once lean back; he still looked out. Through a space in the trees he could see the house door; it was wide open. The little figure dashed up the steps; another figure—a little figure too, slender and young, in its black gown—ran to meet it. It seemed as if they flew together, as Fauntleroy leaped into his mother's arms, hanging about her neck and covering her sweet young face with kisses.

SEVEN

At Church

On the following Sunday morning Mr Mordaunt had a large
congregation. Indeed he could scarcely remember any Sunday
on which the church had been so crowded. People appeared
upon the scene who seldom did him the honour of coming to
hear his sermons. There were even people from Hazelton,
which was the next parish. There were hearty, sunburned
farmers; stout, comfortable, apple-cheeked wives in their best
bonnets and most gorgeous shawls, and half a dozen children
or so to each family. The doctor's wife was there, with her
four daughters. Mrs Kimsey and Mr Kimsey, who kept the
druggist's shop, and made pills, and did up powders for
everybody within ten miles, sat in their pew; Mrs Dibble in
hers, Miss Smiff, the village dressmaker, and her friend Miss
Perkins, the milliner, sat in theirs; the doctor's young man
was present, and the druggist's apprentice; in fact, almost
every family in the countryside was represented in one way or
another.

In the course of the preceding week, many wonderful
stories had been told of little Lord Fauntleroy. Mrs Dibble
had been kept so busy attending to customers who came in to
buy a pennyworth of needles or a ha'p'orth of tape and to
hear what she had to relate, that the little shop-bell over the

door had nearly twinkled itself to death over the coming and going. Mrs Dibble knew exactly how his small lordship's rooms had been furnished for him, what expensive toys had been bought, how there was a beautiful brown pony awaiting him and a small groom to attend it, and a little dog-cart, with silver-mounted harness. And she could tell, too, what all the servants had said when they had caught glimpses of the child on the night of his arrival; and how every female below stairs had said it was a shame, so it was, to part the poor pretty dear from his mother; and had all declared their hearts came into their mouths when he went alone into the library to see his grandfather, for 'there was no knowing how he'd be treated, and his lordship's temper was enough to fluster them with old heads on their shoulders, let alone a child'.

'But if you'll believe me, Mrs Jennifer, mum,' Mrs Dibble had said, 'fear that child does not know—so Mr Thomas hisself says; an' set an' smile he did, an' talked to his lordship as if they'd been friends ever since his first hour. An' the Earl so took aback, Mr Thomas says, that he couldn't do nothing but listen and stare from under his eyebrows. An' it's Mr Thomas's opinion, Mrs Bates, mum, that bad as he is, he was pleased in his secret soul, an' proud too; for a handsomer little fellow, or with better manners, though so old-fashioned, Mr Thomas says, he'd never wish to see.'

And then there had come the story of Higgins. The Reverend Mr Mordaunt had told it at his own dinner table, and the servant who had heard it had told it in the kitchen, and from there it had spread like wildfire.

And on market-day, when Higgins had appeared in town, he had been questioned on every side, and Newick had been questioned too, and in response had shown to two or three people the note signed 'Fauntleroy'.

And so the farmers' wives had found plenty to talk of over their tea and their shopping, and they had done the subject full justice and made the most of it. And on Sunday they had either walked to church or had been driven in their gigs by their husbands, who were perhaps a trifle curious themselves about the new little lord who was to be in time the owner of the soil.

It was by no means the Earl's habit to attend church, but he chose to appear on this first Sunday—it was his whim to present himself in the huge family pew, with Fauntleroy at his side.

There were many loiterers in the churchyard and many lingerers in the lane that morning. There were groups at the gates and in the porch, and there had been much discussion as to whether my lord would really appear or not. When this discussion was at its height, one good woman suddenly uttered an exclamation.

'Eh,' she said, 'that must be the mother, pretty young thing.'

All who had heard turned and looked at the slender figure in black coming up the path. The veil was thrown back from her face and they could see how fair and sweet it was, and how the bright hair curled as softly as a child's under the little widow's cap.

She was not thinking of the people about; she was thinking of Cedric, and of his visits to her, and his joy over his new pony, on which he had actually ridden to her door the day before, sitting very straight and looking very proud and happy. But soon she could not help being attracted by the fact that she was being looked at and that her arrival had created some sort of sensation. She first noticed it because an old woman in a red cloak made a bobbing curtsy to her, and then another did the same thing and said, 'God bless you, my lady!' and one man after another took off his hat as she passed. For a moment she did not understand, and then she realized that it was because she was little Lord Fauntleroy's mother that they did so, and she flushed rather shyly, and smiled and bowed too, and said, 'Thank you,' in a gentle voice to the old woman who had blessed her. To a person who had always lived in a bustling, crowded American city this simple deference was very novel, and at first just a little embarrassing; but after all, she could not help liking and being touched by the friendly warmheartedness of which it seemed to speak. She had scarcely passed through the stone porch into the church before the great event of the day happened. The carriage from the Castle with its handsome horses and tall, liveried servants, bowled round the corner and down the green lane.

'Here they come!' went from one looker-on to another.

And then the carriage drew up, and Thomas stepped down and opened the door, and a little boy, dressed in black velvet, and with a splendid mop of bright waving hair jumped out.

Every man, woman and child looked curiously upon him.

'He's the Captain over again!' said those of the onlookers who remembered his father. 'He's the Captain's self to the life!'

He stood there in the sunlight looking up at the Earl, as Thomas helped that nobleman out, with the most affectionate interest that could be imagined. The instant he could help, he put out his hand and offered his shoulder as if he had been seven feet high. It was plain enough to everyone that however it might be with other people, the Earl of Dorincourt struck no terror into the breast of his grandson.

'Just lean on me,' they heard him say. 'How glad the people are to see you, and how well they all seem to know you!'

'Take off your cap, Fauntleroy,' said the Earl. 'They are bowing to you.'

'To me!' cried Fauntleroy, whipping off his cap in a moment, baring his bright head to the crowd and turning shining, puzzled eyes on them as he tried to bow to everyone at once.

'God bless your lordship!' said the curtsying, red-cloaked old woman who had spoken to his mother; 'long life to you!'

'Thank you, ma'am,' said Fauntleroy. And then they went into the church, and were looked at there, on their way up the aisle to the square red-cushioned and curtained pew.

When Fauntleroy was fairly seated he made two discoveries
which pleased him: the first was that, across the church,
where he could look at her, his mother sat and smiled at him;
the second, that at one end of the pew against the wall knelt
two quaint figures, carven in stone, facing each other as they
kneeled on either side of a pillar supporting two stone mis-
sals, their pointed hands folded as if in prayer, their dress
very antique and strange. On the tablet by them was written
something of which he could only read the curious words:

> Here lyeth ye bodye of Gregorye Arthure Fyrst
> Earle of Dorincort allsoe of Alisone Hildegarde hys
> wyfe.

'May I whisper?' inquired his lordship, devoured by
curiosity.

'What is it?' said his grandfather.

'Who are they?'

'Some of your ancestors,' answered the Earl, 'who lived
a few hundred years ago.'

'Perhaps,' said Lord Fauntleroy, regarding them with
respect, 'perhaps I got my spelling from them.' And then he
proceeded to find his place in the church service. When the
music began he stood up and looked across at his mother,
smiling. He was very fond of music, and his mother and he
often sang together, so he joined in with the rest, his pure,
sweet, high voice rising as clear as the song of a bird. He
quite forgot himself in his pleasure in it. The Earl forgot
himself a little too, as he sat in his curtain-shielded corner of
the pew and watched the boy. Cedric stood with the big
psalter open in his hands, singing with all his childish might,
his face a little uplifted, happily; and as he sang a long ray of
sunshine crept in and slanting through a golden pane of a
stained-glass window brightened the falling hair about his
young head. His mother, as she looked at him across the
church, felt a thrill pass through her heart, and a prayer rose
in it too; a prayer that the pure, simple happiness of his

childish soul might last, and that the strange, great fortune which had fallen to him might bring no wrong or evil with it. There were many soft anxious thoughts in her tender heart in those new days.

'Oh, Ceddie,' she had said to him the evening before, as she hung over him in saying goodnight before he went away, 'oh, Ceddie dear, I wish for your sake I was very clever and could say a great many wise things! But only be good, dear, only be brave, only be kind and true always, and then you will never hurt anyone so long as you live, and you may help many, and the big world may be better because my little child was born. And that is best of all, Ceddie—it is better than everything else, that the world should be a little better because a man has lived—even ever so little better, dearest.'

And on his return to the Castle Fauntleroy had repeated her words to his grandfather.

'And I thought about you when she said that,' he ended; 'and I told her that was the way the world was because you had lived, and I was going to try if I could be like you.'

'And what did she say to that?' asked his lordship a trifle uneasily.

'She said that was right, and we must always look for good in people and try to be like it.'

Perhaps it was this the old man remembered as he glanced through the divided folds of the red curtain of his pew. Many times he looked over the people's heads to where his son's wife sat alone, and he saw the fair face the unforgiven dead had loved, and the eyes which were so like those of the child at his side; but what his thoughts were, and whether they were hard and bitter, or softened a little, it would have been hard to discover.

As they came out of the church, many of those who had attended the service stood waiting to see them pass. As they neared the gate a man who stood with his hat in his hand made a step forward and then hesitated. He was a middle-aged farmer, with a careworn face.

'Well, Higgins,' said the Earl.

Fauntleroy turned quickly to look at him.

'Oh,' he exclaimed, 'is it Mr Higgins?'

'Yes,' answered the Earl dryly; 'and I suppose he came to take a look at his new landlord.'

'Yes, my lord,' said the man, his sunburned face reddening. 'Mr Newick told me his young lordship was kind enough to speak for me, and I thought I'd like to say a word of thanks, if I might be allowed.'

Perhaps he felt some wonder when he saw what a little fellow it was who had innocently done so much for him, and who stood there looking up just as one of his own less fortunate children might have done—apparently not realizing his own importance in the least.

'I've a great deal to thank your lordship for,' he said; 'a great deal. I—'

'Oh,' said Fauntleroy, 'I only wrote the letter. It was my grandfather who did it. But you know how he is about always being good to everybody. Is Mrs Higgins well now?'

Higgins looked a trifle taken aback. He also was somewhat startled at hearing his noble landlord presented in the character of a benevolent being, full of engaging qualities.

'I—well, yes, your lordship,' he stammered; 'the missus is better since the trouble was took off her mind. It was worrying broke her down.'

'I'm glad of that,' said Fauntleroy. 'My grandfather was very sorry about your children having scarlet fever, and so was I. He has had children himself. I'm his son's little boy, you know.'

Higgins was on the verge of being panic-stricken. He felt it would be the safer and more discreet plan not to look at the Earl, as it had been well known that his fatherly affection for his sons had been such that he had seen them about twice a year, and that when they had been ill he had promptly departed for London, because he would not be bored with doctors and nurses. It was a little trying therefore to his lordship's nerves to be told, while he looked on, his eyes gleaming from under his shaggy eyebrows, that he felt an interest in scarlet fever.

'You see, Higgins,' broke in the Earl with a fine grim smile, 'you people have been mistaken in me. Lord Fauntleroy understands me. When you want reliable information on the subject of my character, apply to him. Get into the carriage, Fauntleroy.'

And Fauntleroy jumped in, and the carriage rolled away down the green lane, and even when it turned the corner into the high road the Earl was still grimly smiling.

EIGHT

Learning to Ride

Lord Dorincourt had occasion to wear his grim smile many a time as the days passed by. Indeed, as his acquaintance with his grandson progressed, he wore the smile so often that there were moments when it almost lost its grimness. There is no denying that before Lord Fauntleroy had appeared on the scene the old man had been growing very tired of his loneliness and his gout and his seventy years. After so long a life of excitement and amusement, it was not agreeable to sit alone even in the most splendid room, with one foot on a gout-stool, and with no other diversion than flying into a rage, and shouting at a frightened footman who hated the sight of him. The old Earl was too clever a man not to know perfectly well that his servants detested him, and that even if he had visitors, they did not come for love of him—though some found a sort of amusement in his sharp, sarcastic talk, which spared no one. So long as he had been strong and well, he had gone from one place to another, pretending to amuse himself, though he had not really enjoyed it; and when his health began to fail, he felt tired of everything and shut himself up at Dorincourt with his gout and his newspapers and his books. But he could not read all the time, and he became more and more 'bored', as he called it. He hated the long nights and days, and he grew more and more savage and irritable. And then Fauntleroy came; and when the Earl saw the lad, fortunately for the little fellow, the secret pride of the grandfather was gratified at the outset. If Cedric had been a less handsome little fellow the old man might have taken so strong a dislike to the boy that he would not have given himself the chance to see his grandson's finer qualities. But he chose to think that Cedric's beauty and fearless spirit were the results of Dorincourt blood and a credit to the Dorincourt rank. And then when he heard the lad talk, and saw what a well-bred little fellow he was, notwithstanding his boyish ignorance of all that his new position meant, the old Earl liked his grandson more, and actually began to find himself rather entertained. It had amused him to give into those childish hands the power to bestow a benefit on poor Higgins. My lord cared nothing for poor Higgins, but it pleased him a little that his grandson would be talked about by the country people and would begin to be popular with the tenantry, even in his childhood. Then it had gratified him to drive to church with Cedric and to see excitement and interest caused by the arrival. He knew how the people would speak of the beauty of the little lad; of his fine, strong, straight little body; of his erect bearing, his handsome face and his bright hair, and how they would say (as the Earl had heard one woman exclaim to another) that the boy was 'every inch a lord'. My lord of Dorincourt was an arrogant old man, proud of his name, proud of his rank, and therefore proud to show the world that at last the House of Dorincourt had an heir who was worthy of the position he was to fill.

The morning the new pony had been tried the Earl had been so pleased that he had almost forgotten his gout. When the groom had brought out the pretty creature, which arched its brown glossy neck and tossed its fine head in the sun, the Earl had sat at the open window of the library and had looked on while Fauntleroy took his first riding lesson. He wondered if the boy would show signs of timidity. It was not a very small pony, and he had often seen children lose courage in making their first essay at riding.

Fauntleroy mounted in great delight. He had never been on a pony before, and he was in the highest spirits. Wilkins, the groom, led the animal by the bridle up and down before the library window.

'He's a well plucked 'un, he is,' Wilkins remarked in the stable afterwards with many grins. 'It weren't no trouble to put *him* up. An' a old 'un wouldn't ha' sat any straighter when he *were* up. He ses—ses he to me, "Wilkins," he ses, "am I sitting up straight? They sit up straight at the circus," ses he. And I ses, "As straight as a arrer, your lordship!"—an' he laughs, as pleased as could be, an' he ses, "That's right," he ses, "you tell me if I don't sit up straight, Wilkins." '

But sitting up straight and being led at a walk were not altogether and completely satisfactory. After a few minutes Fauntleroy spoke to his grandfather—watching him from the window.

'Can't I go by myself?' he asked. 'And can't I go faster? The boy on Fifth Avenue used to trot and canter!'

'Do you think you could trot and canter?' said the Earl.

'I should like to try,' answered Fauntleroy.

His lordship made a sign to Wilkins, who at the signal brought up his own horse and mounted it and took Fauntleroy's pony by the leading-rein.

'Now,' said the Earl, 'let him trot.'

The next few minutes were rather exciting to the small equestrian. He found that trotting was not so easy as walking, and the faster the pony trotted, the less easy it was.

'It j-jolts a g-goo-good deal—do-doesn't it?' he said to Wilkins. 'D-does it j-jolt y-you?'

'No, my lord,' answered Wilkins. 'You'll get used to it in time. Rise in your stirrups.'

'I'm ri-rising all the t-time,' said Fauntleroy.

He was both rising and falling rather uncomfortably and with many shakes and bounces. He was out of breath and his face grew red, but he held on with all his might, and sat as straight as he could. The Earl could see that from his window. When the riders came back within speaking distance, after they had been hidden by the trees a few minutes, Fauntleroy's hat was off, his cheeks were like poppies, and his lips were set, but he was still trotting manfully.

'Stop a minute!' said his grandfather. 'Where's your hat?'

Wilkins touched his. 'It fell off, your lordship,' he said with evident enjoyment. 'Wouldn't let me stop to pick it up, my lord.'

'Not much afraid, is he?' asked the Earl dryly.

'Him, your lordship!' exclaimed Wilkins. 'I shouldn't say as he knowed what it meant. I've taught young gen'lemen to ride afore, an' I never see one stick on more determiner.'

'Tired?' said the Earl to Fauntleroy. 'Want to get off?'

'It jolts you more than you think it will,' admitted his young lordship frankly. 'And it tires you a little too; but I don't want to get off. I want to learn how. As soon as I've got my breath I want to go back for the hat.'

The cleverest person in the world, if he had undertaken to teach Fauntleroy how to please the old man who watched him, could not have taught him anything which would have succeeded better. As the pony trotted off again towards the avenue, a faint colour crept up in the fierce old face, and the eyes, under the shaggy brows, gleamed with a pleasure such as his lordship had scarcely expected to know again. And he sat and watched quite eagerly until the sound of the horses' hoofs returned. When they did come, which was after some time, they came at a faster pace. Fauntleroy's hat was still off, Wilkins was carrying it for him; his cheeks were redder than before, and his hair was flying about his ears, but he came at quite a brisk canter.

'There,' he panted as they drew up, 'I c-cantered. I didn't do it as well as the boy on Fifth Avenue, but I did it, and I stayed on!'

He and Wilkins and the pony were close friends after that. Scarcely a day passed on which the country people did not see them out together, cantering gaily on the high road or through the green lanes. The children in the cottages would run to the door to look at the proud little brown pony with the gallant little figure sitting so straight in the saddle, and the young lord would snatch off his cap and swing it at them, and shout, 'Hallo! Good morning!' in a very unlordly manner, though with great heartiness. Sometimes he would stop and talk with the children, and once Wilkins came back to the Castle with a story of how Fauntleroy had insisted on dismounting near the village school, so that a boy who was lame and tired might ride home on his pony.

'An' I'm blessed,' said Wilkins, in telling the story at the stables, 'I'm blessed if he'd hear of anything else! He wouldn't let me get down, because he said the boy mightn't feel comfortable on a big horse. An' ses he, "Wilkins," ses he, "that boy's lame and I'm not, and I want to talk to him too." And up the lad has to get, and my lord trudges alongside of him with his hands in his pockets, and his cap on the back of his head, a-whistling and talking as easy as you please! And when we come to the cottage, an' the boy's mother come out all in a taking to see what's up, he whips off his cap an' ses he, "I've brought your son home, ma'am," ses he, "because his leg hurt him, and I don't think that stick is enough for him to lean on; and I'm going to ask my grandfather to have a pair of crutches made for him." An' I'm blest if the woman wasn't struck all of a heap, as well she might be! I thought I should 'a' hex-plodid, myself!'

When the Earl heard the story he was not angry, as Wilkins had been half afraid that he would be; on the contrary, he laughed outright, and called Fauntleroy up to him, and made him tell all about the matter from beginning to end, and then he laughed again. And actually, a few days later, the Dorincourt carriage stopped in the green lane before the cottage where the lame boy lived, and Fauntleroy jumped out and walked up to the door, carrying a pair of strong, light, new crutches, shouldered like a gun, and presented them to Mrs Hartle (the lame boy's name was Hartle) with these words: 'My grandfather's compliments, and if you please, these are for your boy, and we hope he will get better.'

'I said your compliments,' he explained to the Earl when he returned to the carriage. 'You didn't tell me to, but I thought perhaps you forgot. That was right, wasn't it?'

And the Earl laughed again, and did not say it was not. In fact, the two were becoming more intimate every day, and every day Fauntleroy's faith in his lordship's benevolence and virtue increased. He had no doubt whatever that his grandfather was the most amiable and generous of elderly gentlemen. Certainly he himself found his wishes gratified almost before they were uttered; and such gifts and pleasures were lavished upon him, that he was sometimes almost bewildered by his own possessions. Apparently he was to have everything he wanted, and to do everything he wished to do. And though this would certainly not have been a very wise plan to pursue with all small boys, his young lordship bore it amazingly well. Perhaps, notwithstanding his sweet nature, he might have been somewhat spoiled by it, if it had not been for the hours he spent with his mother at Court Lodge. That 'best friend' of his watched over him very closely and tenderly. The two had many long talks together, and he never went back to the Castle with her kisses on his cheeks without carrying in his heart some simple, pure words worth remembering.

There was one thing, it is true, which puzzled the little fellow very much. He thought over the mystery of it much oftener than anyone supposed; even his mother did not know how often he pondered on it; the Earl for a long time never suspected that he did so at all. But being quick to observe, the little boy could not help wondering why it was that his mother and grandfather never seemed to meet. He had noticed that they never did meet. When the Dorincourt carriage stopped at Court Lodge the Earl never alighted, and on the rare occasions of his lordship's going to church, Fauntleroy was always left to speak to his mother in the porch alone, or perhaps to go home with her. And yet, every day, fruit and flowers were sent to Court Lodge from the hothouses at the Castle. But the one virtuous action of the Earl's which had set him upon the pinnacle of perfection in Cedric's eyes, was what he had done soon after that first Sunday when Mrs Errol had walked home from church unattended. About a week later, when Cedric was going one day to visit his mother, he found at the door, instead of the large carriage and prancing pair, a pretty little brougham and a handsome bay horse.

'That is a present from you to your mother,' the Earl said abruptly. 'She cannot go walking about the country. She needs a carriage. The man who drives will take charge of it. It is a present from *you*.'

Fauntleroy's delight could but feebly express itself. He could scarcely contain himself until he reached the lodge. His mother was gathering roses in the garden. He flung himself out of the little brougham and flew to her.

'Dearest!' he cried. 'Could you believe it? This is yours! He says it is a present from me. It is your own carriage to drive everywhere in!'

He was so happy that she did not know what to say. She could not have borne to spoil his pleasure by refusing to accept the gift, even though it came from the man who chose to consider himself her enemy. She was obliged to step into the carriage, roses and all, and let herself be taken for a drive, while Fauntleroy told her stories of his grandfather's goodness and amiability. They were such innocent stories that sometimes she could not help laughing a little, and then she would draw her little boy closer to her side and kiss him, feeling glad that he could see only good in the old man who had so few friends.

The very next day after that, Fauntleroy wrote to Mr Hobbs. He wrote quite a long letter, and after the first copy was written, he brought it to his grandfather to be inspected.

'Because,' he said, 'it's so uncertain about the spelling. And if you'll tell me the mistakes, I'll write it out again.'

This was what he had written:

My dear mr hobbs i want to tell you about my granfarther he is the best earl you ever new it is a mistake about earls being tirents he is not a tirent at all i wish you new him you would be good friends i am sure you would he has the gout in his foot and is a grate sufrer but he is so pashent i love him more every day becaus no one could help loving an earl that who is kind to every one in this world i wish you could talk to him he knows everything in the world you can ask him any question but he has never plaid base ball he has given me a pony and cart and my mamma a bewtifle carige and i have three rooms and toys of all kinds it would serprise you you would like the castle and the park it is such a large castle you could lose yourself wilkins tells me wilkins is my groom he says there is a dungon under the castle it is so pretty every thing in the park would serprise you there are such big trees and there are deers and rabbits and games flying about in the cover my grandfarther is very rich but he is not proud and orty as you thought earls always were i like to be with him the people are so polite and kind they take of their hats to you and the women make curtsies and sometimes say god bless you i can ride now but at first it shook me when I troted my grandfarther let a poor man stay on his farm when he could not pay his rent and mrs mellon went to take wine and things to his sick children i should like to see you and i wish dearest could live at the castle but i am very happy when i don't miss her too much and i love my grandfarther every one does plees write soon.

your afechshnet old friend
CEDRIC ERROL

ps no one is in the dungon my granfarther never had any one langwishin in there
ps he is such a good earl he reminds me of you he is a unerversle favrit

'Do you miss your mother very much?' asked the Earl when he had finished reading this.

'Yes,' said Fauntleroy, 'I miss her all the time.'

He went and stood before the Earl and put his hand on his knee looking up at him.

'*You* don't miss her, do you?' he said.

'I don't know her,' answered his lordship rather crustily.

'I know that,' said Fauntleroy, 'and that's what makes me wonder. She told me not to ask you any questions, and—and I won't, but sometimes I can't help thinking, you know, and it makes me all puzzled. But I'm not going to ask any questions. And when I miss her very much, I go and look out of my window to where I see her light shine for me every night through an open place in the trees. It is a long way off, but she puts it in her window as soon as it is dark and I can see it twinkle far away, and I know what it says.'

'What does it say?' asked my lord.

'It says, "Good night, God keep you all the night!" —just what she used to say when we were together. Every night she used to say that to me, and every morning she said, "God bless you all the day!" So you see I am quite safe all the time—'

'Quite, I have no doubt,' said his lordship dryly. And he drew down his beetling eyebrows and looked at the little boy so fixedly and so long that Fauntleroy wondered what he could be thinking of.

NINE

The Poor Cottages

The fact was, his lordship the Earl of Dorincourt thought in those days of many things of which he had never thought before, and all his thoughts were in one way or another connected with his grandson. His pride was the strongest part of his nature, and the boy gratified it at every point. Through this pride he began to find a new interest in life. He began to take pleasure in showing his heir to the world. The world had known of his disappointment in his sons; so there was an agreeable touch of triumph in exhibiting this new Lord Fauntleroy, who could disappoint no one. He wished the child to appreciate his own power and to understand the splendour of his position; he wished that others should realize it too. He made plans for his future. Sometimes in secret he actually found himself wishing that his own past life had been a better one, and that there had been less in it that this pure, childish heart would shrink from if it knew the truth. It was not agreeable to think how the beautiful innocent face would look if its owner should be made by any chance to understand that his grandfather had been called for many a year 'the wicked Earl of Dorincourt'. The thought even made him feel a trifle nervous. He did not wish the boy to find it out. Sometimes in this new interest he forgot his gout, and after a while his doctor was surprised to find his noble patient's health growing better than he had expected it ever would be again. Perhaps the Earl grew better because the time did not pass so slowly for him, and he had something to think of besides his pains and infirmities.

One fine morning people were amazed to see little Lord Fauntleroy riding his pony with another companion than Wilkins. This new companion rode a tall, powerful, grey horse, and was no other than the Earl himself. It was in fact Fauntleroy who had suggested this plan. As he had been on the point of mounting his pony he had said rather wistfully to his grandfather:

'I wish you were going with me. When I go away I feel lonely because you are left all by yourself in such a big castle. I wish you could ride too.'

And the greatest excitement had been aroused in the stables a few minutes later by the arrival of an order that Selim was to be saddled for the Earl. After that Selim was saddled almost every day; and the people became accustomed to the sight of the tall grey horse carrying the tall grey old man with his handsome, fierce, eagle face, by the side of the brown pony which bore little Lord Fauntleroy. And in their rides together through the green lanes and pretty country roads, the two riders became more intimate than ever. And gradually the old man heard a great deal about 'Dearest' and her life. As Fauntleroy trotted by the big horse he chatted gaily. There could not well have been a brighter little comrade, his nature was so happy. It was he who talked the most. The Earl often was silent, listening and watching the joyous, glowing face. Sometimes he would tell his young companion to set the pony off at a gallop, and when the little fellow dashed off, sitting so straight and fearless, he would watch the boy with a gleam of pride and pleasure in his eyes; and Fauntleroy when, after such a dash, he came back waving his cap with a laughing shout, always felt that he and his grandfather were very good friends indeed.

One thing that the Earl discovered was that his son's

wife did not lead an idle life. It was not long before he learned that the poor people knew her very well indeed. When there was sickness or sorrow or poverty in any house, the little brougham often stood before the door.

'Do you know,' said Fauntleroy once, 'they all say, "God bless you!" when they see her, and the children are glad. There are some who go to her house to be taught to sew. She says she feels so rich now that she wants to help the poor ones.'

It had not displeased the Earl to find that the mother of his heir had a beautiful young face and looked as much like a lady as if she had been a duchess, and in one way it did not displease him to know that she was popular and beloved by the poor. And yet he was often conscious of a hard, jealous pang when he saw how she filled her child's heart and how the boy clung to her as his best beloved. The old man would have desired to stand first himself and have no rival.

That same morning he drew up his horse on an elevated point of the moor over which they rode, and made a gesture with his whip, over the broad, beautiful landscape spread before them.

'Do you know that all that land belongs to me?' he said to Fauntleroy.

'Does it?' answered Fauntleroy. 'How much it is to belong to one person, and how beautiful!'

'Do you know that some day it will all belong to you— that and a great deal more?'

'To me!' exclaimed Fauntleroy in rather an awestricken voice. 'When?'

'When I am dead,' his grandfather answered.

'Then I don't want it,' said Fauntleroy; 'I want you to live always.'

'That's kind,' answered the Earl in his dry way; 'nevertheless some day it will all be yours—some day you will be the Earl of Dorincourt.'

Little Lord Fauntleroy sat very still in his saddle for a few moments. He looked over the broad moors, the green farms, the beautiful copses, the cottages in the lanes, the pretty villages, and over the trees to where the turrets of the great castle rose, grey and stately. Then he gave a queer little sigh.

'What are you thinking of?' asked the Earl.

'I am thinking,' replied Fauntleroy, 'what a little boy I am, and of what Dearest said to me.'

'What was it?' inquired the Earl.

'She said that perhaps it was not so easy to be very rich; that if anyone had so many things always, one might sometimes forget that everyone else was not so fortunate, and that one who is rich should always be careful and try to remember. I was talking to her about how good you were, and she said that was such a good thing, because an earl had so much power, and if he cared only about his own pleasure and never thought about the people who lived on his lands, they might have trouble that he could help—and there were so many people, and it would be such a hard thing. And I was just looking at all those houses, and thinking how I should have to find out about the people when I was an earl. How did you find out about them?'

As his lordship's knowledge of his tenantry consisted in finding out which of them paid their rent promptly, and in turning out those who did not, this was rather a hard question. 'Newick finds out for me,' he said, and he pulled his great grey moustache, and looked at his small questioner rather uneasily.

'We will go home now,' he added; 'and when you are an earl, see to it that you are a better one than I have been!'

He was very silent as they rode home. He felt it to be almost incredible that he, who had never really loved anyone in his life, should find himself growing so fond of this little fellow—as without doubt he was. At first he had only been pleased and proud of Cedric's beauty and bravery, but there was something more than pride in his feeling now. He laughed a grim, dry laugh all to himself sometimes, when he thought how he liked to have the boy near him, how he liked to hear his voice, and how in secret he really wished to be liked and thought well of by his small grandson.

'I'm an old fellow in my dotage, and I have nothing else to think of,' he would say to himself; and yet he knew it was not that altogether. And if he allowed himself to admit the truth, he would perhaps have found himself obliged to own that the very things which attracted him, in spite of himself, were the qualities he had never possessed—the frank, true, kindly nature, the affectionate trustfulness which could never think evil.

It was only about a week after that ride when, after a visit to his mother, Fauntleroy came into the library with a troubled, thoughtful face. He sat down in that high-backed chair in which he had sat on the evening of his arrival, and for a while he looked at the embers on the hearth. The Earl watched him in silence, wondering what was coming. It was evident that Cedric had something on his mind. At last he looked up. 'Does Newick know all about the people?' he asked.

'It is his business to know about them,' said his lordship. 'Been neglecting it—has he?'

Contradictory as it may seem, there was nothing which entertained and edified him more than the little fellow's interest in his tenantry. He had never taken any interest in them himself, but it pleased him well enough that, with all his childish habits of thought and in the midst of all his childish amusements and high spirits, there should be such a quaint seriousness working in the curly head.

'There is a place,' said Fauntleroy, looking up at him with wide-open, horror-stricken eyes. 'Dearest has seen it; it is at the other end of the village. The houses are close together, and almost falling down; you can scarcely breathe; and the people are so poor, and everything is dreadful! Often they have fever and the children die; and it makes them wicked to live like that, and be so poor and miserable! It is worse than Michael and Bridget! The rain comes in at the roof! Dearest went to see a poor woman who lived there. She would not let me come near her until she had changed all her things. The tears ran down her cheeks when she told me about it!'

The tears had come into his own eyes, but he smiled through them.

'I told her you didn't know, and I would tell you,' he said. He jumped down and came and leaned against the Earl's chair. 'You can make it all right,' he said, 'just as you made it all right for Higgins. You always make it all right for everybody. I told her you would, and that Newick must have forgotten to tell you.'

The Earl looked down at the hand on his knee. Newick had not forgotten to tell him; in fact, Newick had spoken to him more than once of the desperate condition of the end of the village known as Earl's Court. He knew all about the tumbledown, miserable cottages, and the bad drainage, and the damp walls and broken windows and leaking roofs, and all about the poverty, the fever and the misery. Mr Mordaunt had painted it all to him in the strongest words he could use, and his lordship had used violent language in response; and, when his gout had been at the worst, he had said that the sooner the people of Earl's Court died and were buried by the parish the better it would be—and there was an end of the matter. And yet, as he looked at the small hand on his knee, and from the small hand to the honest, earnest, frank-eyed face, he was actually a little ashamed both of Earl's Court and of himself.

'What!' he said. 'You want to make a builder of model cottages of me, do you?' And he positively put his own hand upon the childish one and stroked it.

'Those must be pulled down,' said Fauntleroy with great eagerness. 'Dearest says so. Let us—let us go and have them pulled down tomorrow. The people will be so glad when they see you! They'll know you have come to help them!' And his eyes shone like stars in his glowing face.

The Earl rose from his chair and put his hand on the child's shoulder. 'Let us go out and take our walk on the terrace,' he said with a short laugh, 'and we can talk it over.'

And though he laughed two or three times again, as they walked to and fro on the broad stone terrace, where they walked together almost every fine evening, he seemed to be thinking of something which did not displease him, and still he kept his hand on his small companion's shoulder.

TEN

The Earl Alarmed

The truth was that Mrs Errol had found a great many sad things in the course of her work among the poor of the little village that appeared so picturesque when it was seen from the moor-sides. Everything was not as picturesque when seen near by, as it looked from a distance. She had found idleness and poverty and ignorance where there should have been comfort and industry. And she had discovered after a while that Erlesboro was considered to be the worst village in that part of the country. Mr Mordaunt had told her a great many of his difficulties and discouragements, and she had found out a great deal by herself. The agents who had managed the property had always been chosen to please the Earl, and had cared nothing for the degradation and wretchedness of the poor tenants. Many things, therefore, had been neglected which should have been attended to, and matters had gone from bad to worse.

As to Earl's Court, it was a disgrace, with its dilapidated houses and miserable, careless, sickly people. When first Mrs Errol went to the place, it made her shudder. Such ugliness and slovenliness and want seemed worse in a country place than in a city. It seemed as if there it might be helped. And as she looked at the squalid, uncared-for children growing up in

117

the midst of vice and brutal indifference, she thought of her own little boy spending his days in the great, splendid castle, guarded and served like a young prince, having no wish ungratified, and knowing nothing but luxury and ease and beauty. And a bold thought came into her wise little mother-heart. Gradually she had begun to see, as had others, that it had been her boy's good fortune to please the Earl very much, and that he would scarcely be likely to be denied anything for which he expressed a desire.

'The Earl would give him everything,' she said to Mr Mordaunt. 'He would indulge his every whim. Why should not that indulgence be used for the good of others? It is for me to see that this shall come to pass.'

She knew she could trust the kind, childish heart; so she told the little fellow the story of Earl's Court, feeling sure that he would speak of it to his grandfather, and hoping that some good results would follow.

And strange as it appeared to everyone, good results did follow. The fact was that the strongest power to influence the Earl was his grandson's perfect confidence in him—the fact that Cedric always believed that his grandfather was going to do what was right and generous. He could not quite make up his mind to let him discover that he had no inclination to be generous at all, and that he wanted his own way on all occasions, whether it was right or wrong. It was such a novelty to be regarded with admiration as a benefactor of the entire human race and the soul of nobility, that he did not enjoy the idea of looking into the affectionate brown eyes and saying 'I am a violent, selfish old rascal; I never did a generous thing in my life, and I don't care about Earl's Court or the poor people'—or something which would amount to the same thing. He actually had learned to be fond enough of that small boy with the mop of yellow love-locks, to feel that he himself would prefer to be guilty of an amiable action now and then. And so—though he laughed at himself—after some reflection, he sent for Newick, and had quite a long interview with him on the subject of the Court, and it was decided that the wretched hovels should be pulled down and new houses should be built.

'It is Lord Fauntleroy who insists on it,' he said dryly; 'he thinks it will improve the property. You can tell the tenants that it's his idea.' And he looked down at his small lordship, who was lying on the hearthrug playing with Dougal. The great dog was the lad's constant companion, and followed him about everywhere, stalking solemnly after him when he walked, and trotting majestically behind when he rode or drove.

Of course both the country people and the town people heard of the proposed improvement. At first many of them would not believe it; but when a small army of workmen arrived and commenced pulling down the crazy, squalid cottages, people began to understand that little Lord Fauntleroy had done them a good turn again, and that through his innocent interference the scandal of Earl's Court had at last been removed. If he had only known how they talked about him and praised him everywhere, and prophesied great things for him when he grew up, how astonished he would have been! But he never suspected it. He lived his simple, happy child life, frolicking about in the park; chasing the rabbits to their burrows; lying under the trees on the grass, or on the rug in the library, reading wonderful books and talking to the Earl about them, and then telling the stories again to his mother; writing long letters to Dick and Mr Hobbs, who responded in characteristic fashion; riding out at his grandfather's side, or with Wilkins as escort. As they rode through the market town he used to see the people turn and look, and he noticed that as they lifted their hats their faces often brightened very much, but he thought it was all because his grandfather was with him.

'They are so fond of you,' he once said, looking up at his lordship with a bright smile. 'Do you see how glad they are when they see you? I hope they will some day be as fond of me. It must be nice to have *every*body like you.'

And he felt quite proud to be the grandson of so greatly admired and beloved an individual.

When the cottages were being built, the lad and his grandfather used to ride over to Earl's Court together to look at them, and Fauntleroy was full of interest. He would dismount from his pony and go and make acquaintance with the workmen, asking them questions about building and bricklaying, and telling them things about America. After two or three such conversations, he was able to enlighten the Earl on the subject of brickmaking as they rode home.

'I always like to know about things like those,' he said, 'because you never know what you are coming to.'

When he left them the workmen used to talk him over among themselves, and laugh at his odd, innocent speeches; but they liked him and liked to see him stand among them, talking away, with his hands in his pockets, his hat pushed back on his curls, and his small face full of eagerness. 'He's a rare 'un,' they used to say. 'An' a noice little outspoken chap too. Not much o' th' bad stock in him.' And they would go home and tell their wives about him, and the women would tell each other, and so it came about that almost everyone talked of, or knew some story of, little Lord Fauntleroy; and gradually almost everyone knew that the 'wicked Earl' had found something he cared for at last—something which had touched and even warmed his hard, bitter old heart.

But no one knew quite how much it had been warmed, and how day by day the old man found himself caring more and more for the child, who was the only creature that had ever trusted him. He found himself looking forward to the time when Cedric would be a young man, strong and beautiful, with life all before him, but having still that kind heart and the power to make friends everywhere; and the Earl wondered what the lad would do, and how he would use his gifts. Often as he watched the little fellow lying upon the hearth, conning some big book, the light shining on the bright young head, his old eyes would gleam and his cheek would flush.

'The boy can do anything,' he would say to himself, 'anything!'

He never spoke to anyone else of his feeling for Cedric; when he spoke of him to others it was always with the same grim smile. But Fauntleroy soon knew that his grandfather loved him and always liked him to be near—near to his chair if they were in the library, opposite to him at table or by his side when he rode or drove or took his evening walk on the broad terrace.

'Do you remember,' Cedric said once, looking up from his book as he lay on the rug, 'do you remember what I said to you that first night about our being good companions? I don't think any people could be better friends than we are, do you?'

'We are pretty good companions, I should say,' replied his lordship. 'Come here.'

Fauntleroy scrambled up and went to him.

'Is there anything you want?' the Earl asked. 'Anything you have not?'

The little fellow's brown eyes fixed themselves on his grandfather with a rather wistful look.

'Only one thing,' he answered.

'What is that?' inquired the Earl.

Fauntleroy was silent a second. He had not thought matters over to himself so long for nothing.

'What is it?' my lord repeated.

Fauntleroy answered.

'It is Dearest,' he said.

The old Earl winced a little.

'But you see her almost every day,' he said. 'Is not that enough?'

'I used to see her all the time,' said Fauntleroy. 'She used to kiss me when I went to sleep at night, and in the morning she was always there, and we could tell each other things without waiting.'

The old eyes and young ones looked into each other through a moment of silence. Then the Earl knitted his brows.

'Do you *never* forget about your mother?' he said.

'No,' answered Fauntleroy, 'never; and she never forgets about me. I shouldn't forget about *you* you know, if I didn't live with you. I should think about you all the more.'

'Upon my word,' said the Earl, after looking at him a moment longer, 'I believe you would!'

The jealous pang that came when the boy spoke so of his mother seemed even stronger than it had been before—it was stronger because of this old man's increasing affection for the boy.

But it was not long before he had other pangs, so much harder to face that he almost forgot, for the time, he had ever hated his son's wife at all. And in a strange and startling way it happened. One evening, just before the Earl's Court cottages were completed, there was a grand dinner party at Dorincourt. There had not been such a party at the Castle for a long time. A few days before it took place, Sir Harry Lorridaile and Lady Lorridaile, who was the Earl's only sister, actually came for a visit—a thing which caused the greatest excitement in the village and set Mrs Dibble's shop-bell tinkling madly again, because it was well known that Lady Lorridaile had only been to Dorincourt once since her marriage, thirty-five years before. She was a handsome old lady with white curls and dimpled, peachy cheeks, and she was as good as gold, but she had never approved of her brother any more than did the rest of the world, and having a strong will of her own and not being at all afraid to speak her mind frankly, she had, after several lively quarrels with his lordship, seen very little of him since her young days.

She had heard a great deal of him that was not pleasant through the years in which they had been separated. She had heard about his neglect of his wife, and of the poor lady's death; and of his indifference to his children; and of the two weak, vicious, unprepossessing elder boys who had been no credit to him or to anyone else. Those two elder sons, Bevis and Maurice, she had never seen; but once there had come to Lorridaile Park a tall, stalwart, beautiful young fellow about eighteen years old who had told her that he was her nephew Cedric Errol, and that he had come to see her because he was passing near the place and wished to look at his Aunt Constantia, of whom he had heard his mother speak. Lady Lorridaile's kind heart had warmed through and through at the sight of the young man, and she had made him stay with her a week, and petted him and made much of him and admired him immensely. He was so sweet-tempered, light-hearted, spirited a lad, that when he went away she had hoped to see him often again; but she never did, because the Earl had been in a bad humour when he went back to Dorincourt, and had forbidden him ever to go to Lorridaile Park again. But Lady Lorridaile had always remembered him tenderly, and though she feared he had made a rash marriage in America, she had been very angry when she heard how he had been cast off by his father and that no one really knew where or how he lived. At last there came a rumour of his death, and then Bevis had been thrown from his horse and killed, and Maurice had died in Rome of the fever; and soon after came the story of the American child who was to be found and brought home as Lord Fauntleroy.

'Probably to be ruined as the others were,' she said to her husband, 'unless his mother is good enough and has a will of her own to help her to take care of him.'

But when she heard that Cedric's mother had been parted from him she was almost too indignant for words.

'It is disgraceful, Harry!' she said. 'Fancy a child of that age being taken from his mother, and made the companion of a man like my brother! The old Earl will either be brutal to the boy or indulge him until he is a little monster. If I thought it would do any good to write—'

'It wouldn't, Constantia,' said Sir Harry.

'I know it wouldn't,' she answered. 'I know his lordship the Earl of Dorincourt too well; but it is outrageous.'

Not only the poor people and farmers heard about little

Lord Fauntleroy; others knew of him. He was talked about so much and there were so many stories of him—of his beauty, his sweet temper, his popularity and his growing influence over the Earl his grandfather—that rumours of him reached the gentry at their country places and he was heard of in more than one county of England. People talked about him at the dinner tables, ladies pitied his young mother, and wondered if the boy were as handsome as he was said to be, and men who knew the Earl and his habits laughed heartily at the stories of the little fellow's belief in his lordship's amiability. Sir Thomas Asshe of Asshaine Hall, being in Erlesboro one day, met the Earl and his grandson riding together and stopped to shake hands with my lord and congratulate him on his change of looks and on his recovery from the gout. 'And d'ye know,' he said, when he spoke of the incident afterwards, 'the old man looked as proud as a turkey-cock; and upon my word I don't wonder, for a handsomer, finer lad than his grandson I never saw! As straight as a dart, and sat his pony like a young trooper!'

And so by degrees Lady Lorridaile, too, heard of the child; she heard about Higgins, and the lame boy, and the cottages at Earl's Court, and a score of other things—and she began to wish to see the little fellow. And just as she was wondering how it might be brought about, to her utter astonishment, she received a letter from her brother inviting her to come with her husband to Dorincourt.

'It seems incredible!' she exclaimed. 'I have heard it said that the child has worked miracles, and I begin to believe it. They say my brother adores the boy and can scarcely endure to have him out of sight. And he is so proud of him! Actually I believe he wants to show him to us.' And she accepted the invitation at once.

When she reached Dorincourt Castle with Sir Harry, it was late in the afternoon, and she went to her room at once before seeing her brother. Having dressed for dinner she entered the drawing-room. The Earl was there standing near the fire and looking very tall and imposing; and at his side stood a little boy in black velvet, and a large Vandyke collar of rich lace—a little fellow whose round bright face was so handsome, and who turned upon her such beautiful, candid brown eyes, that she almost uttered an exclamation of pleasure and surprise at the sight.

As she shook hands with the Earl, she called him by the name she had not used since her girlhood.

'What, Molyneux,' she said, 'is this the child?'

'Yes. Constantia,' answered the Earl, 'this is the boy. Fauntleroy, this is your grand-aunt, Lady Constantia Lorridaile.'

'How do you do, grand-aunt?' said Fauntleroy.

Lady Lorridaile put her hand on his shoulder, and after looking down into his upraised face a few seconds, kissed him warmly.

'I am your Aunt Constantia,' she said, 'and I loved your poor papa, and you are very like him.'

'It makes me glad when I am told I am like him,' answered Fauntleroy, 'because it seems as if everyone liked him—just like Dearest, eszackly—Aunt Constantia' (adding the two words after a second's pause).

Lady Lorridaile was delighted. She bent and kissed him again, and from that moment they were warm friends.

'Well, Molyneux,' she said aside to the Earl afterwards, 'it could not possibly be better than this!'

'I think not,' answered his lordship dryly. 'He is a fine little fellow. We are great friends. He believes me to be the most charming and sweet-tempered of philanthropists. I will confess to you, Constantia—as you would find it out if I did not—that I am in some slight danger of becoming rather an old fool about him.'

'What does his mother think of you?' asked Lady Lorridaile, with her usual straightforwardness.

'I have not asked her,' answered the Earl, slightly scowling.

'Well,' said Lady Lorridaile, 'I will be frank with you at the outset, Molyneux, and tell you I don't approve of your course, and that it is my intention to call on Mrs Errol as soon as possible; so if you wish to quarrel with me you had better mention it at once. What I hear of the young creature makes me quite sure that the child owes her everything. We were told even at Lorridaile Park that your poorer tenants adore her already.'

'They adore *him*,' said the Earl, nodding towards Fauntleroy. 'As to Mrs Errol, you'll find her a pretty little woman. I'm rather in debt to her for giving some of her beauty to the boy, and you can go to see her if you like. All I ask is that she will remain at Court Lodge, and that you will not ask me to go and see her,' and he scowled a little again.

'But he doesn't hate her as much as he used to, that is plain enough to me,' her ladyship said to Sir Harry afterwards. 'And he is a changed man in a measure, and, incredible as it may seem, Harry, it is my opinion that he is being made into a human being, through nothing more or less than his affection for that innocent, affectionate little fellow. Why, the child actually loves him—leans on his chair and against his knees. My lord's own children would as soon have thought of nestling up to a tiger.'

The very next day she went to call upon Mrs Errol. When she returned she said to her brother:

'Molyneux, she is the loveliest little woman I ever saw! She has a voice like a silver bell, and you may thank her for making the boy what he is. She has given him more than her beauty, and you make a great mistake in not persuading her to come and take charge of you. I shall invite her to Lorridaile.'

'She'll not leave the boy,' replied the Earl.

'I must have the boy too,' said Lady Lorridaile, laughing.

But she knew Fauntleroy would not be given up to her, and each day she saw more clearly how closely those two had grown to each other, and how all the proud, grim old man's ambition and hope and love centred themselves in the child, and how the warm, innocent nature returned his affection with most perfect trust and faith.

She knew too that the prime reason for the great dinner party was the Earl's secret desire to show the world his grandson and heir; and to let people see that the boy who had been so much spoken of and described was even a finer little specimen of boyhood than rumour had made him.

'Bevis and Maurice were such a bitter humiliation to him,' she said to her husband. 'Everyone knew it. He actually hated them. His pride has full sway here.' Perhaps there was not one person who accepted the invitation without feeling some curiosity about little Lord Fauntleroy, and wondering if he would be on view.

And when the time came he was on view.

'The lad has good manners,' said the Earl. 'He will be in no one's way. Children are usually idiots or bores—mine were both—but he can actually answer when he's spoken to, and be silent when he is not. He is never offensive.'

But he was not allowed to be silent very long. Everyone had something to say to him. The fact was they wished to make him talk. The ladies petted him and asked him questions and the men asked him questions too, and joked with him, as the men on the steamer had done when he crossed the Atlantic. Fauntleroy did not quite understand why they laughed so sometimes when he answered them, but he was so used to seeing people amused when he was quite serious, that he did not mind. He thought the whole evening delightful. The magnificent rooms were so brilliant with lights, there were so many flowers, the gentlemen seemed so gay, and the ladies wore such beautiful, wonderful dresses, and such sparkling ornaments in their hair and on their necks. There was one young lady who, he heard them say, had just come down from London, where she had spent 'the season'; and she was so charming that he could not keep his eyes from her. She was a rather tall young lady, with a proud little head and very soft hair, and large eyes the colour of purple pansies, and the colour of her cheeks and lips was like that of a rose. She was dressed in a beautiful white dress, and had pearls around her throat. There was one strange thing about this young lady. So many gentlemen stood near her, and seemed anxious to please her, that Fauntleroy thought she must be something like a princess. He was so much interested in her that without knowing it he drew nearer and nearer to her and at last she turned and spoke to him.

'Come here, Lord Fauntleroy,' she said, smiling; 'and tell me why you look at me so.'

'I was thinking how beautiful you are,' his young lordship replied.

Then all the gentlemen laughed outright, and the young lady laughed a little too, and the rose colour in her cheeks brightened.

'Ah, Fauntleroy,' said one of the gentlemen who had laughed most heartily, 'make the most of your time! When you are older you will not have the courage to say that.'

'But nobody could help saying it,' said Fauntleroy sweetly. 'Could you help it? Don't *you* think she is pretty too?'

'We are not allowed to say what we think,' said the gentleman, while the rest laughed more than ever.

But the beautiful young lady—her name was Miss Vivian Herbert—put out her hand and drew Cedric to her side, looking prettier than before, if possible.

'Lord Fauntleroy shall say what he thinks,' she said; 'and I am much obliged to him. I am sure he thinks what he says.' And she kissed him on his cheek.

'I think you are prettier than anyone I ever saw,' said Fauntleroy, looking at her with innocent, admiring eyes, 'except Dearest. Of course, I couldn't think anyone *quite* as pretty as Dearest. I think she is the prettiest person in the world.'

'I am sure she is,' said Miss Vivian Herbert. And she laughed and kissed his cheek again.

She kept him by her side a great part of the evening, and the group of which they were the centre was very gay. He did not know how it happened, but before long he was telling them all about America, and the Republican rally, and Mr Hobbs and Dick, and in the end he proudly produced from his pocket Dick's parting gift—the red silk handkerchief.

'I put it in my pocket tonight because it was a party,' he said. 'I thought Dick would like me to wear it at a party.'

And queer as the big, flaming, spotted thing was, there was a serious, affectionate look in his eyes, which prevented his audience from laughing very much.

'You see I like it,' he said, 'because Dick is my friend.'

But though he was talked to so much, as the Earl had said, he was in no one's way. He could be quiet and listen when others talked, and so no one found him tiresome. A slight smile crossed more than one face when several times he went and stood near his grandfather's chair, or sat on a stool close to him, watching him and absorbing every word he uttered with the most charmed interest. Once he stood so near the chair's arm that his cheek touched the Earl's shoulder, and his lordship, detecting the general smile, smiled a little himself. He knew what the lookers-on were thinking, and he felt some secret amusement in their seeing what a good friend he was to this youngster, who might have been expected to share the popular opinion of him.

Mr Havisham had been expected to arrive in the afternoon, but, strange to say, he was late. Such a thing had really never been known to happen before during all the years in which he had been a visitor at Dorincourt Castle. He was so late that the guests were on the point of rising to go in to dinner when he arrived. When he approached his host the Earl regarded him with amazement. He looked as if he had been hurried or agitated; his dry, keen old face was actually pale.

'I was detained,' he said, in a low voice to the Earl, 'by—an extraordinary event.'

It was as unlike the methodic old lawyer to be agitated by anything as it was to be late, but it was evident that he had been disturbed. At dinner he ate scarcely anything, and two or three times, when he was spoken to, he started as if his thoughts were far away. At dessert, when Fauntleroy came in, he looked at him more than once, nervously and uneasily. Fauntleroy noted the look and wondered at it. He and Mr

Havisham were on friendly terms, and they usually exchanged smiles.

The lawyer seemed to have forgotten to smile that evening.

The fact was he forgot everything but the strange and painful news he knew he must tell the Earl before the night was over—the strange news which he knew would be so terrible a shock, and which would change the face of everything. As he looked about at the splendid rooms and the brilliant company—at the people gathered together, he knew, more that they might see the bright-haired little fellow near the Earl's chair than for any other reason—as he looked at the proud old man and at little Lord Fauntleroy smiling at his side, he really felt quite shaken, notwithstanding that he was a hardened old lawyer. What a blow it was that he must deal them!

He did not exactly know how the long superb dinner ended. He sat through it as if he were in a dream, and several times he saw the Earl glance at him in surprise.

But it was over at last, and the gentlemen joined the ladies in the drawing-room. They found Fauntleroy sitting on a sofa with Miss Vivian Herbert—the great beauty of the last London season; they had been looking at some pictures, and he was thanking his companion, as the door opened.

'I'm ever so much obliged to you for being so kind to me!' he was saying; 'I never was at a party before, and I've enjoyed myself so much!'

He had enjoyed himself so much that when the gentlemen gathered about Miss Herbert again and began to talk to her, as he listened and tried to understand their laughing speeches his eyelids began to droop. They drooped until they covered his eyes two or three times, and then the sound of Miss Herbert's low, pretty laugh would bring him back, and he would open them again for about two seconds. He was quite sure he was not going to sleep, but there was a large, yellow satin cushion behind him and his head sank against it, and after a while his eyelids drooped for the last time. They did not even quite open when, as it seemed a long time after, someone kissed him lightly on the cheek. It was Miss Vivian Herbert, who was going away, and she spoke to him softly.

'Good night, little Lord Fauntleroy,' she said. 'Sleep well.'

And in the morning he did not know that he had tried to open his eyes and had murmured sleepily:

'Good night—I'm so—glad—I saw you—you are so—pretty—'

He only had a very faint recollection of hearing the gentlemen laugh again and of wondering why they did it.

No sooner had the last guest left the room than Mr Havisham turned from his place by the fire, and stepped nearer the sofa, where he stood looking down at the sleeping occupant. Little Lord Fauntleroy was taking his ease luxuriously. One leg crossed the other and swung over the edge of the sofa; one arm was flung easily above his head; the warm flush of healthy, happy, childish sleep was on his quiet face; his waving tangle of bright hair strayed over the yellow satin cushion. He made a picture well worth looking at.

As Mr Havisham looked at it, he put his hand up and rubbed his shaven chin, with a harassed countenance.

'Well, Havisham,' said the Earl's harsh voice behind him. 'What is it? It is evident something has happened. What was the extraordinary event, if I may ask?'

Mr Havisham turned from the sofa, still rubbing his chin.

'It was bad news,' he answered, 'distressing news, my lord—the worst of news. I am sorry to be the bearer of it.'

The Earl had been uneasy for some time during the evening, as he glanced at Mr Havisham, and when he was uneasy he was always ill-tempered.

'Why do you look so at the boy!' he exclaimed irritably. 'You have been looking at him all the evening as if— See here now, why should you look at the boy, Havisham, and hang over him like some bird of ill-omen! What has your news to do with Lord Fauntleroy?'

'My lord,' said Mr Havisham, 'I will waste no words. My news has everything to do with Lord Fauntleroy. And if we are to believe it—it is not Lord Fauntleroy who lies sleeping before us, but only the son of Captain Errol. And the present Lord Fauntleroy is the son of your son Bevis, and is at this moment in a lodging-house in London.'

The Earl clutched the arms of his chair with both his hands until the veins stood out upon them; the veins stood out on his forehead too; his fierce old face was almost livid.

'What do you mean!' he cried out. 'You are mad! Whose lie is this?'

'If it is a lie,' answered Mr Havisham, 'it is painfully like the truth. A woman came to my chambers this morning. She said your son Bevis married her six years ago in London. She showed me her marriage certificate. They quarrelled a year after the marriage, and he paid her to keep away from him. She has a son five years old. She is an American of the lower class—an ignorant person—and until lately she did not fully understand what her son could claim. She consulted a lawyer, and found out that the boy was really Lord Fauntleroy and the heir to the earldom of Dorincourt; and she, of course, insists on his claims being acknowledged.'

There was a movement of the curly head on the yellow satin cushion. A soft, long, sleepy sigh came from the parted lips, and the little boy stirred in his sleep, but not at all restlessly or uneasily. Not at all as if his slumber were disturbed by the fact that he was being proved a small impostor and that he was not Lord Fauntleroy at all and never would be the Earl of Dorincourt. He only turned his rosy face more on its side as if to enable the old man who stared at it so solemnly to see it better.

The handsome, grim old face was ghastly. A bitter smile fixed itself upon it.

'I should refuse to believe a word of it,' he said, 'if it were not such a low, scoundrelly piece of business that it becomes quite possible in connection with the name of my son Bevis. It is quite like Bevis. He was always a disgrace to us. Always a weak, untruthful, vicious young brute with low tastes—my son and heir, Bevis, Lord Fauntleroy. The woman is an ignorant, vulgar person, you say?'

'I am obliged to admit that she can scarcely spell her own name,' answered the lawyer. 'She is absolutely uneducated and openly mercenary. She cares for nothing but the money. She is very handsome in a coarse way, but—'

The fastidious old lawyer ceased speaking and gave a sort of shudder.

The veins on the old Earl's forehead stood out like purple cords. Something else stood out upon it too—cold drops of moisture. He took out his handkerchief and swept them away. His smile grew even more bitter.

'And I,' he said, 'I objected to—to the other woman, the mother of this child'—pointing to the sleepy form on the sofa—'I refused to recognize her. And yet she could spell her own name. I suppose this is retribution.'

Suddenly he sprang up from his chair and began to walk up and down the room. Fierce and terrible words poured forth from his lips. His rage and hatred and cruel disappointment shook him as a storm shakes a tree. His violence was something dreadful to see, and yet Mr Havisham noticed that at the very worst of his wrath he never seemed to forget the little sleeping figure on the yellow satin cushions, and that he never once spoke loud enough to awaken it.

'I might have known it,' he said. 'They were a disgrace to me from their first hour! I hated them both; and they hated me! Bevis was the worst of the two. I will not believe this yet though! I will contend against it to the last. But it is like Bevis—it is like him!'

And then he raged again and asked questions about the woman, about her proofs, and pacing the room, turned first white and then purple in his repressed fury.

When at last he had learned all there was to be told, and knew the worst, Mr Havisham looked at him with a feeling of anxiety. He looked broken and haggard and changed. His rages had always been bad for him, but this one had been worse than the rest because there had been something more than rage in it.

He came slowly back to the sofa, at last, and stood near it.

'If anyone had told me I could be fond of a child,' he said, his harsh voice low and unsteady, 'I should not have believed them. I always detested children—my own more than the rest. I am fond of this one; he is fond of me' (with a bitter smile). 'I am not popular; I never was. But he is fond of me. He never was afraid of me—he always trusted me. He would have filled my place better than I have filled it. I know that. He would have been an honour to the name.'

He bent down and stood a minute or so looking at the happy, sleeping face. His shaggy eyebrows were knitted fiercely, and yet somehow he did not seem fierce at all. He put up his hand, pushed the bright hair back from the forehead, and then turned away and rang the bell.

When the largest footman appeared, he pointed to the sofa.

'Take,' he said, and then his voice changed a little, 'take Lord Fauntleroy to his room.'

ELEVEN

Anxiety in America

When Mr Hobbs's young friend left him to go to Dorincourt Castle and become Lord Fauntleroy, and the grocery-man had time to realize that the Atlantic Ocean lay between himself and the small companion who had spent so many agreeable hours in his society, he really began to feel very lonely indeed. The fact was, Mr Hobbs was not a clever man, nor even a bright one; he was indeed rather a slow and heavy person, and he had never made many acquaintances. He was not mentally energetic enough to know how to amuse himself, and in truth he never did anything of an entertaining nature but read the newspapers and add up his accounts. It was not very easy for him to add up his accounts, and sometimes it took him a long time to bring them out right; and in the old days little Lord Fauntleroy, who had learned how to add up quite nicely with his fingers and a slate and pencil, had sometimes even gone to the length of trying to help him; and then too he had been so good a listener and had taken such an interest in what the newspaper said, and he and Mr Hobbs had held such long conversations about the Revolution and the British and the elections and the Republican party, that it was no wonder his going left a blank in the grocery store. At first it seemed to Mr Hobbs that Cedric was not really far away, and would come back again; that some day he would look up from his paper and see the lad standing in the doorway, in his white suit and red stockings, and with his straw hat on the back of his head, and would hear him say in his cheerful little voice: 'Hallo, Mr Hobbs! This is a hot day—isn't it?' But as the days passed on and this did not happen, Mr Hobbs felt very dull and uneasy. He did not even enjoy his newspaper as much as he used to. He would put the paper down on his knee after reading it, and sit and stare at the high stool for a long time. There were some marks on the long legs which made him feel quite dejected and melancholy. They were marks made by the heels of the next Earl of Dorincourt, when he kicked and talked at the same time. It seems that even youthful earls kick the legs of things they sit on; noble blood and lofty lineage do not prevent it. After looking at those marks Mr Hobbs would take out his gold watch and open it and stare at the inscription: 'From his oldest friend, Lord Fauntleroy, to Mr Hobbs. When this you see, remember me.' And after staring at it awhile he would shut it up with a loud snap, and sigh and get up and go and stand in the doorway—between the box of potatoes and the barrel of apples—and look up the street. At night, when the store was closed, he would light his pipe and walk slowly along the pavement until he reached the house where Cedric had lived, on which there was a sign that read, 'This House to Let'; and he would stop near it and look up and shake his head, and puff at his pipe very hard, and after a while walk mournfully back again.

This went on for two or three weeks before any new idea came to him. Being slow and ponderous, it always took him a long time to reach a new idea. As a rule he did not like new ideas, but preferred old ones. After two or three weeks, however, during which, instead of getting better, matters really grew worse, a novel plan slowly and deliberately dawned upon him. He would go to see Dick. He smoked a great many pipes before he arrived at the conclusion, but finally he did arrive at it. He would go to see Dick. He knew all about

Dick. Cedric had told him, and his idea was that perhaps Dick might be some comfort to him in the way of talking things over.

So one day when Dick was very hard at work blacking a customer's boots, a short stout man with a heavy face and a bald head stopped on the pavement and stared for two or three minutes at the boot-black's sign, which read:

PROFESOR DICK TIPTON
CAN'T BE BEAT.

He stared at it so long that Dick began to take a lively interest in him, and when he had put the finishing touch to his customer's boots he said:

'Want a shine, sir?'

The stout man came forward deliberately and put his foot on the rest.

'Yes,' he said.

Then, when Dick fell to work, the stout man looked from Dick to the sign and from the sign to Dick.

'Where did you get that?' he asked.

'From a friend o' mine,' says Dick, 'a little feller. He guv' me the whole outfit. He was the best little feller ye ever saw. He's in England now. Gone to be one o' those lords.'

'Lord—Lord,' asked Mr Hobbs, with ponderous slowness, 'Lord Fauntleroy—goin' to be Earl of Dorincourt?'

Dick almost dropped his brush.

'Why, boss,' he exclaimed, 'd'ye know him yerself?'

'I've known him,' answered Mr Hobbs, wiping his warm forehead, 'ever since he was born. We were lifetime acquaintances—that's what *we* were.'

It really made him feel quite agitated to speak of it. He pulled the splendid, gold watch out of his pocket and opened it, and showed the inside of the case to Dick.

' "When this you see, remember me",' he read. 'That was his parting keepsake to me. "I don't want you to forget me"—those were his words—I'd ha' remembered him,' he went on, shaking his head, 'if he hadn't given me a thing, an' I hadn't seen hide nor hair on him again. He was a companion as *any* man would remember.'

'He was the nicest little feller I ever see,' said Dick. 'An' as to sand—I never ha' seen so much sand to a little feller. I thought a heap o' him, I did—an' we was friends too—we was sort o' chums frum the fust, that little 'un an' me. I grabbed his ball from under a stage fur him, an' he never forgot it; an' he'd come down here, he would, with his mother or his nuss, an' he'd holler: "Hallo, Dick!" at me, as friendly as if he was six feet high, when he warn't knee high to a grasshopper, and was dressed in gal's clo'es. He was a gay little chap, and when you was down on your luck it did you good to talk to him.'

'That's so,' said Mr Hobbs. 'It was a pity to make an earl out of him. He would have *shone* in the grocery business—or dry goods either; he would have *shone*!' And he shook his head with deeper regret than ever.

It proved that they had so much to say to each other that it was not possible to say it all at one time, and so it was agreed that the next night Dick should make a visit to the store and keep Mr Hobbs company. The plan pleased Dick well enough. He had been a street waif nearly all his life, but he had never been a bad boy, and he had always had a private yearning for a more respectable kind of existence. Since he had been in business for himself, he had made enough money to enable him to sleep under a roof instead of out in the streets, and he had begun to hope he might reach even a higher plane in time. So, to be invited to call on a stout, respectable man who owned a corner store, and even had a horse and wagon, seemed to him quite an event.

'Do you know anything about earls and castles?' Mr Hobbs inquired. 'I'd like to know more of the particulars.'

'There's a story of some on 'em in the *Penny Story Gazette*,' said Dick. 'It's called the "Crime of a Coronet; or, the Revenge of the Countess May". It's a boss thing too. Some of us boys 're takin' it to read.'

'Bring it up when you come,' said Mr Hobbs, 'an' I'll pay for it. Bring all you can find that have any earls in 'em. If there aren't earls, markises'll do, or dooks—though *he* never made mention of any dooks or markises. We did go over coronets a little, but I never happened to see any. I guess they don't keep 'em 'round here.'

'Tiffany 'd have 'em if anybody did,' said Dick, 'but I don't know as I'd know one if I saw it.'

Mr Hobbs did not explain that he would not have known one if he saw it. He merely shook his head ponderously.

'I s'pose there is very little call for 'em,' he said, and that ended the matter.

This was the beginning of quite a substantial friendship. When Dick went up to the store Mr Hobbs received him with great hospitality. He gave him a chair tilted against the door, near a barrel of apples, and after his young visitor was seated, he made a jerk at them with the hand in which he held his pipe, saying:

'Help yourself.'

Then he looked at the story papers, and after that they read and discussed the British aristocracy; and Mr Hobbs smoked his pipe very hard and shook his head a great deal. He shook it most when he pointed out the high stool with the marks on its legs.

'There's his very kicks,' he said impressively; 'his very kicks. I sit and look at 'em by the hour. This is a world of ups an' it's a world of downs. Why, he'd set there, and eat biscuits out of a box, an' apples out of a barrel, an' pitch his cores into the street; an' now he's a lord a-livin' in a castle. Those are a lord's kicks; they'll be an earl's kicks some day. Sometimes I says to myself, says I, "Well, I'll be jiggered!" '

He seemed to derive a great deal of comfort from his reflections and Dick's visit. Before Dick went home they had a supper in the small back room; they had biscuits and cheese and sardines, and other canned things out of the store, and Mr Hobbs solemnly opened two bottles of ginger ale, and pouring out two glasses, proposed a toast.

'Here's to *him*!' he said, lifting his glass, 'an' may he teach 'em a lesson—earls an' markises an' dooks an' all!'

After that night the two saw each other often, and Mr Hobbs was much more comfortable and less desolate. They read the *Penny Story Gazette* and other interesting things, and gained a knowledge of the habits of the nobility and gentry which would have surprised those despised classes if they had realized it. One day Mr Hobbs made a pilgrimage to a bookstore down town for the express purpose of adding to their library. He went to a clerk and leaned over the counter to speak to him.

'I want,' he said, 'a book about earls.'

'What!' exclaimed the clerk.

'A book,' repeated the grocery-man, 'about earls.'

'I'm afraid,' said the clerk, looking rather queer, 'that we haven't what you want.'

'Haven't?' said Mr Hobbs anxiously. 'Well, say markises then—or dooks.'

'I know of no such book,' answered the clerk.

Mr Hobbs was much disturbed. He looked down at the floor, then he looked up.

'None about female earls?' he inquired.

'I'm afraid not,' said the clerk with a smile.

'Well,' exclaimed Mr Hobbs, 'I'll be jiggered!'

He was just going out of the store, when the clerk called him back and asked him if a story in which the nobility were chief characters would do. Mr Hobbs said it would—if he could not get an entire volume devoted to earls. So the clerk sold him a book called *The Tower of London*, written by Mr Harrison Ainsworth, and he carried it home.

When Dick came they began to read it. It was a very wonderful and exciting book, and the scene was laid in the reign of the famous English queen who is called by some people Bloody Mary. And as Mr Hobbs heard of Queen Mary's deeds and the habit she had of chopping people's heads off, putting them to the torture and burning them alive he became very much excited. He took his pipe out of his

mouth and stared at Dick, and at last he was obliged to mop
the perspiration from his brow with his red pocket-handkerchief.

'Why, he ain't safe!' he said. 'He ain't safe! If the
women folks can sit up on their thrones an' give the word for
things like that to be done, who's to know what's happening
to him this very minute? He's no more safe than nothing! Just
let a woman like that get mad, an' no one's safe!'

'Well,' said Dick, though he looked rather anxious himself, 'ye see this 'ere 'un isn't the one that's bossin' things
now. I know her name's Victohry, an' this 'un here in the
book—her name's Mary.'

'So it is,' said Mr Hobbs, still mopping his forehead,
'so it is. An' the newspapers are not sayin' anything about
any racks, thumbscrews or stake-burnin's—but still it doesn't
seem as if 'twas safe for him over there with those queer
folks. Why, they tell me they don't keep the Fourth o' July!'

He was privately uneasy for several days; and it was not
until he received Fauntleroy's letter and had read it several
times, both to himself and to Dick, and had also read the
letter Dick got about the same time, that he became com-
posed again.

But they both found great pleasure in their letters. They
read and reread them, and talked them over and enjoyed
every word of them. And they spent days over the answers
they sent, and read them over almost as often as the letters
they had received.

It was rather a labour for Dick to write his. All his
knowledge of reading and writing he had gained during a few
months when he had lived with his elder brother, and had
gone to a night school; but, being a sharp boy, he had made
the most of that brief education, and had spelled out things in
newspapers since then, and practised writing with bits of
chalk on pavements or walls or fences. He told Mr Hobbs all
about his life and about his elder brother, who had been
rather good to him after their mother died, when Dick was
quite a little fellow. Their father had died some time before.
The brother's name was Ben, and he had taken care of Dick

as well as he could, until the boy was old enough to sell newspapers and run errands. They had lived together, and as he grew older Ben had managed to get along until he had quite a decent place in a store.

'And then,' exclaimed Dick with disgust, 'blest if he didn't go an' marry a gal! Just went and got spoony, an' hadn't any more sense left! Married her, an' set up house-keepin' in two back rooms. An' a hefty 'un she was, a regular tiger-cat. She'd tear things to pieces when she got mad—and she was mad *all* the time. Had a baby just like her—yell day 'n' night! An' if I didn't have to 'tend it, an' when it screamed, she'd fire things at me. She fired a plate at me one day an' hit the baby—cut its chin. Doctor said he'd carry the mark till he died. A nice mother she was! Crackey! but didn't we have a time—Ben 'n' mehself 'n' the young 'un. She was mad at Ben because he didn't make money faster; 'n' at last he went out West with a man to set up a cattle ranch. An' he hadn't been gone a week 'fore, one night, I got home from sellin' my papers, 'n' the rooms wus locked up 'n' empty, 'n' the woman o' the house, she told me Minna'd gone—shown a clean pair o' heels. Some 'un else said she'd gone across the water to be nuss to a lady as had a little baby too. Never heard a word of her since—nuther has Ben. If I'd ha bin him, I wouldn't ha' fretted a bit—'n' I guess he didn't. But he thought a heap o' her at the start. Tell you, he was spoons on her. She was a daisy-lookin' gal, too, when she was dressed up 'n' not mad. She'd big black eyes 'n' black hair down to her knees; she'd make it into a rope as big as your arm, and twist it 'round 'n' 'round her head; 'n' I tell you her eyes'd snap! Folks used to say she was part *I*tali-un—said her mother or father'd come from there, 'n' it made her queer. I tell ye she was one of 'em—she was!'

He often told Mr Hobbs stories of her and of his brother Ben, who, since his going out West, had written once or twice to Dick. Ben's luck had not been good, and he had wandered from place to place; but at last he had settled on a ranch in California, where he was at work at the time when Dick became acquainted with Mr Hobbs.

'That gal,' said Dick one day, 'she took all the grit out o' him. I couldn't help feeling sorry for him sometimes.'

They were sitting in the store doorway together, and Mr Hobbs was filling his pipe.

'He oughtn't to 'ave married,' he said solemnly as he rose to get a match. 'Women—I never could see any use in 'em myself.'

As he took the match from its box, he stopped and looked down on the counter.

'Why,' he said, 'if here isn't a letter! I didn't see it afore. The postman must have laid it down when I wasn't noticin', or the newspaper slipped over it.'

He picked it up and looked at it carefully.

'It's from *him*!' he exclaimed. 'That's the very one it's from!'

He forgot his pipe altogether. He went back to his chair quite excited, and took his pocket-knife and opened the envelope.

'I wonder what news there is this time,' he said.

And then he unfolded the letter and read as follows:

DORINCOURT CASTLE
My dear Mr Hobbs,—i write this in a great hury becaus i have something curous to tell you i know you will be very much suprised my dear frend when i tel you. It is all a mistake and i am not a lord and I shall not have to be an earl there is a lady whitch was marid to my uncle bevis who is dead and she has a little boy and he is lord fauntleroy because that is the way it is in England the earls eldest sons little boy is the earl if every body is dead i mean if his farther and grandfarther are dead my grandfarther is not dead but my uncle bevis is and so his boy is lord Fauntleroy and i am not becaus my papa was the youngest son and my name is Cedric Errol like it was when I was in

New York and all the things will belong to the other
boy i thought at first i should have to give him my
pony and cart but my grandfarther says i need not my
grandfarther is very sorry and i think he does not like
the lady but preaps he thinks dearest and i are sorry
becaus i shall not be an earl i would like to be an earl
now better than i thout i would at first becaus this is a
beautifle castle and i like every body so and when you
are rich you can do so many things i am not rich now
becaus when your papa is only the youngest son he is
not very rich i am going to learn to work so that I can
take care of dearest i have been asking Wilkins about
grooming horses preaps i might be a groom or a
coachman, the lady brought her little boy to the castle
and my grandfarther and Mr Havisham talked to her i
think she was angry she talked loud and my grandfarther
was angry too i never saw him angry before i wish it
did not make them all mad i thort i would tell you and
Dick right away becaus you would be intrusted so no
more at present with love from

　　　　　　　your old frend
　　　　CEDRIC ERROL (Not lord Fauntleroy)

Mr Hobbs fell back in his chair, the letter dropped on his
knee, his penknife slipped to the floor and so did the envelope.

'Well,' he ejaculated, 'I am jiggered!'

He was so dumbfounded that he actually changed his
exclamation. It had always been his habit to say, 'I *will* be
jiggered,' but this time he said, 'I *am* jiggered.' Perhaps he
really *was* jiggered. There is no knowing.

'Well,' said Dick, 'the whole thing's bust up, hasn't it?'

'Bust!' said Mr Hobbs. 'It's my opinion it's all a put-up
job o' the British 'ristycrats to rob him of his rights because
he's an American. They've had a spite agin us ever since the
Revolution, an' they're takin' it out on him. I told you he
wasn't safe, an' see what's happened! Like as not, the whole
government's got together to rob him of his lawful ownin's.'

He was very much agitated. He had not approved of the change in his young friend's circumstances at first, but lately he had become more reconciled to it, and after the receipt of Cedric's letter he had perhaps even felt some secret pride in his young friend's magnificence. He might not have a good opinion of earls, but he knew that even in America money was considered rather an agreeable thing, and if all the wealth and grandeur were to go with the title, it must be rather hard to lose it.

'They're trying to rob him,' he said, 'that's what they're doing, and folks that have money ought to look after him.'

And he kept Dick with him until quite a late hour to talk it over, and when that young man left he went with him to the corner of the street; and on his way back he stopped opposite the empty house for some time, staring at the 'To Let', and smoking his pipe in much disturbance of mind.

TWELVE

The Rival Claimants

A very few days after the dinner party at the Castle, almost everybody in England who read the newspapers at all knew the romantic story of what had happened at Dorincourt. It made a very interesting story when it was told with all the details. There was the little American boy who had been brought to England to be Lord Fauntleroy, and who was said to be so fine and handsome a little fellow, and to have already made people fond of him; there was the old Earl, his grandfather, who was so proud of his heir; there was the pretty young mother who had never been forgiven for marrying Captain Errol; and there was the strange marriage of Bevis, the dead Lord Fauntleroy, and the strange wife, of whom no one knew anything, suddenly appearing with her son, and saying that he was the real Lord Fauntleroy and must have his rights. All these things were talked about and written about, and caused a tremendous sensation. And then there came the rumour that the Earl of Dorincourt was not satisfied with the turn affairs had taken, and would perhaps contest the claim by law, and the matter might end with a wonderful trial.

There never had been such excitement before in the county in which Erlesboro was situated. On market-days people stood in groups and talked and wondered what would be done; the farmers' wives invited one another to tea that they might tell one another all they had heard and all they thought and all they thought other people thought. They related wonderful anecdotes about the Earl's rage and his determination not to acknowledge the new Lord Fauntleroy, and his hatred of the woman who was the claimant's mother. But of course it was Mrs Dibble who could tell the most, and who was more in demand than ever.

'An' a bad look-out it is,' she said. 'An' if you were to ask me, ma'am, I should say as it was a judgement on him for the way he's treated that sweet young cre'tur as he parted from her child—for he's got that fond of him an' that set on him an' that proud on him as he's a'most drove mad by what's happened. An' what's more, this new one's no lady, as his little lordship's ma is. She's a bold-faced, black-eyed thing, as Mr Thomas says no gentleman in livery 'u'd be-mean hisself to be guv orders by; an' let her come into the house, he says, an' he goes out of it. An' the boy don't no more compare with the other one than nothin' you could mention. An' mercy knows what's goin' to come of it all, an' where it's to end, an' you might have knocked me down with a feather when Jane brought the news.'

In fact there was excitement everywhere; at the Castle, in the library, where the Earl and Mr Havisham sat and talked; in the servants' hall, where Mr Thomas and the butler and the other men and women servants gossiped and ex-claimed at all times of the day; and in the stables, where Wilkins went about his work in a quite depressed state of mind, and groomed the brown pony more beautifully than ever, and said mournfully to the coachman that he 'never taught a young gen'leman to ride as took to it more nat'ral or was a better-plucked one than he was. He was a one as it were some pleasure to ride behind.'

But in the midst of all this disturbance there was one person who was quite calm and untroubled. That person was the little Lord Fauntleroy who was said not to be Lord

Fauntleroy at all. When first the state of affairs had been explained to him, he had felt some little anxiousness and perplexity, it is true, but its foundation was not in baffled ambition.

While the Earl told him what had happened, he had sat on a stool holding on to his knee, as he so often did when he was listening to anything interesting; and by the time the story was finished he looked quite sober.

'It makes me feel very queer,' he said; 'it makes me feel—queer!'

The Earl looked at the boy in silence. It made him feel queer too—queerer than he had ever felt in his whole life. And he felt more queer still when he saw that there was a troubled expression on the small face which was usually so happy.

'Will they take Dearest's house away from her— and her carriage?' Cedric asked in a rather unsteady, anxious little voice.

'No!' said the Earl decidedly—in quite a loud voice in fact. 'They can take nothing from her.'

'Ah,' said Cedric with evident relief. 'Can't they?'

Then he looked up at his grandfather, and there was a wistful shade in his eyes, and they looked very big and soft.

'That other boy,' he said rather tremulously, 'he will have to—to be your boy now—as I was—won't he?'

'No!' answered the Earl—and he said it so fiercely and loudly that Cedric jumped.

'No?' he exclaimed in wonderment. 'Won't he? I thought—'

He stood up from his stool quite suddenly.

'Shall I be your boy, even if I'm not going to be an earl?' he said. 'Shall I be your boy, just as I was before?' And his flushed little face was all alight with eagerness.

How the old Earl did look at him from his head to foot, to be sure! How his great shaggy brows did draw themselves together, and how queerly his deep eyes shone under them— how very queerly!

'My boy!' he said—and, if you'll believe it, his very voice was queer, almost shaky and a little broken and hoarse, not at all what you would expect an earl's voice to be, though he spoke more decidedly and peremptorily even than before. 'Yes, you'll be my boy as long as I live; and by George, sometimes I feel as if you were the only boy I had ever had.'

Cedric's face turned red to the roots of his hair; it turned red with relief and pleasure. He put both his hands deep into his pockets and looked squarely into his noble relative's eyes.

'Do you?' he said. 'Well then, I don't care about the earl part at all. I don't care whether I'm an earl or not. I thought—you see, I thought the one that was going to be the earl would have to be your boy, too, and—and I couldn't be. That was what made me feel so queer.'

The Earl put his hand on his shoulder and drew him nearer.

'They shall take nothing from you that I can hold for you,' he said, drawing his breath hard. 'I won't believe yet that they can take anything from you. You were made for the place, and—well, you may fill it still. But whatever comes, you shall have all that I can give you—all!'

It scarcely seemed as if he were speaking to a child, there was such determination in his face and voice; it was more as if he were making a promise to himself—and perhaps he was.

He had never before known how deep a hold upon him his fondness for the boy and his pride in him had taken. He had never seen his strength and good qualities and beauty as he seemed to see them now. To his obstinate nature it seemed impossible—more than impossible— to give up what he had so set his heart upon. And he had determined that he would not give it up without a fierce struggle.

Within a few days after she had seen Mr Havisham, the woman who claimed to be Lady Fauntleroy presented herself at the Castle, and brought her child with her. She was sent away. The Earl would not see her, she was told by the footman at the door; his lawyer would attend to her case. It was Thomas who gave the message, and who expressed his opinion of her freely afterwards, in the servants' hall. He 'hoped' he said, 'as he had wore livery in 'igh famblies long enough to know a lady when he see one, an' if that was a lady he was no judge of females'.

'The one at the Lodge,' added Thomas loftily, ' 'Merican or no 'Merican, she's one o' the right sort, as any gentleman u'd reckinize with 'alf a heye. I remarked it myself to Henry when fust we called there.'

The woman drove away; the look on her handsome common face half frightened, half fierce. Mr Havisham had noticed, during his interviews with her, that though she had a passionate temper and a coarse, insolent manner, she was neither so clever nor so bold as she meant to be; seemed sometimes to be almost overwhelmed by the position in which she had placed herself. It was as if she had not expected to meet with such opposition.

'She is evidently,' the lawyer said to Mrs Errol, 'a person from the lower walks of life. She is uneducated and untrained in everything, and quite unused to meeting people like ourselves on any terms of equality. She does not know what to do. Her visit to the Castle quite cowed her. She was infuriated, but she was cowed. The Earl would not receive her, but I advised him to go with me to the Dorincourt Arms, where she is staying. When she saw him enter the room, she turned white, though she flew into a rage at once, and threatened and demanded in one breath.'

The fact was that the Earl had stalked into the room and stood, looking like a venerable aristocratic giant, staring at the woman from under his beetling brows, and not condescending a word. He simply stared at her, taking her in from head to foot as if she were some repulsive curiosity. He let her talk and demand until she was tired without himself uttering a word, and then he said:.

'You say you are my eldest son's wife. If that is true, and if the proof you offer is too much for us, the law is on your side. In that case your boy is Lord Fauntleroy. The matter will be sifted to the bottom, you may rest assured. If your claims are proved, you will be provided for. I want to see nothing either of you or the child as long as I live. The place will unfortunately have enough of you after my death. You are exactly the kind of person I should have expected my son Bevis to choose.'

And then he turned his back upon her and stalked out of the room as he had stalked into it.

Not many days after that a visitor was announced to Mrs Errol, who was writing in her little morning-room. The maid who brought the message looked rather excited; her eyes were quite round with amazement in fact, and being young and inexperienced, she regarded her mistress with nervous sympathy.

'It's the Earl hisself, ma'am!' she said in tremulous awe.

When Mrs Errol entered the drawing-room a very tall, majestic-looking old man was standing on the tiger-skin rug. He had a handsome, grim old face, with an aquiline profile, a long white moustache and an obstinate look.

'Mrs Errol, I believe?' he said.

'Mrs Errol,' she answered.

'I am the Earl of Dorincourt,' he said.

He paused a moment, almost unconsciously, to look into her uplifted eyes. They were so like the big, affectionate, childish eyes he had seen uplifted to his own so often every day during the last few months, that they gave him a quite curious sensation.

'The boy is very like you,' he said abruptly.

'It has been often said so, my lord,' she replied, 'but I have been glad to think him like his father also.'

As Lady Lorridaile had told him, her voice was very sweet, and her manner was very simple and dignified. She did not seem in the least troubled by his sudden coming.

'Yes,' said the Earl, 'he is like—my son—too.' He put his hand up to his big white moustache and pulled it fiercely. 'Do you know,' he said, 'why I have come here?'

'I have seen Mr Havisham,' Mrs Errol began, 'and he has told me of the claims which have been made—'

'I have come to tell you,' said the Earl, 'that they will be investigated and contested, if a contest can be made. I have come to tell you that the boy shall be defended with all the power of the law. His rights—'

The soft voice interrupted him.

'He must have nothing that is *not* his by right, even if the law can give it to him,' she said.

'Unfortunately the law cannot,' said the Earl. 'If it could it should. This outrageous woman and her child—'

'Perhaps she cares for him as much as I care for Cedric, my lord,' said little Mrs Errol. 'And if she was your eldest son's wife, her son is Lord Fauntleroy, and mine is not.'

She was no more afraid of him than Cedric had been, and she looked at him just as Cedric would have looked, and he, having been an old tyrant all his life, was privately pleased by it. People so seldom dared to differ from him that there was an entertaining novelty in it.

'I suppose,' he said, scowling slightly, 'that you would much prefer that he should not be the Earl of Dorincourt?'

Her fair young face flushed.

'It is a very magnificent thing to be the Earl of Dorincourt, my lord,' she said. 'I know that, but I care most that he should be what his father was—brave and just and true always.'

'In striking contrast to what his grandfather was, eh?' said his lordship sardonically.

'I have not had the pleasure of knowing his grandfather,' replied Mrs Errol, 'but I know my little boy believes—' She stopped short a moment, looking quietly into his face, and then she added: 'I know that Cedric loves you.'

'Would he have loved me,' said the Earl dryly, 'if you had told him why I did not receive you at the Castle?'

'No,' answered Mrs Errol; 'I think not. That was why I did not wish him to know.'

'Well,' said my lord brusquely, 'there are few women who would not have told him.'

He suddenly began to walk up and down the room, pulling his great moustache more violently than ever.

'Yes, he is fond of me,' he said, 'and I am fond of him. I can't say I ever was fond of anything before. I am fond of him. He pleased me from the first. I am an old man, and was tired of my life. He has given me something to live for, I am proud of him. I was satisfied to think of his taking his place some day as the head of the family.'

He came back and stood before Mrs Errol.

'I am miserable,' he said. 'Miserable!'

He looked as if he was. Even his pride could not keep his voice steady or his hands from shaking. For a moment it almost seemed as if his deep, fierce eyes had tears in them. 'Perhaps it is because I am miserable that I have come to you,' he said, quite glaring down at her. 'I used to hate you; I have been jealous of you. This wretched, disgraceful business has changed that. After seeing that repulsive woman who calls herself the wife of my son Bevis, I actually felt it would be a relief to look at you. I have been an obstinate old fool, and I suppose I have treated you badly. You are like the boy, and the boy is the first object in my life. I am miserable, and I came to you merely because you are like the boy, and he cares for you, and I care for him. Treat me as well as you can, for the boy's sake.'

He said it all in his harsh voice, and almost roughly, but somehow he seemed so broken down for the time that Mrs Errol was touched to the heart. She got up and moved an armchair a little forward.

'I wish you would sit down,' she said in a soft, pretty, sympathetic way. 'You have been so much troubled that you are very tired, and you need all your strength.'

It was just as new to him to be spoken to and cared for in that gentle, simple way as it was to be contradicted. He was reminded of 'the boy' again, and he actually did as she asked him. Perhaps his disappointment and wretchedness were good discipline for him; if he had not been wretched he might have continued to hate her, but just at present he found her a little soothing. Almost anything would have seemed pleasant by contrast with Lady Fauntleroy; and this one had so sweet a face and voice, and a pretty dignity when she spoke or moved. Very soon, by the quiet magic of these influences, he began to feel less gloomy, and then he talked still more.

'Whatever happens,' he said, 'the boy shall be provided for. He shall be taken care of, now and in the future.'

Before he went away he glanced around the room.

'Do you like the house?' he demanded.

'Very much,' she answered.

'This is a cheerful room,' he said. 'May I come here again and talk this matter over?'

'As often as you wish, my lord,' she replied.

And then he went out to his carriage and drove away, Thomas and Henry almost stricken dumb upon the box at the turn affairs had taken.

THIRTEEN

Dick to the Rescue

Of course as soon as the story of Lord Fauntleroy and the difficulties of the Earl of Dorincourt were discussed in the English newspapers, they were discussed in the American newspapers. The story was too interesting to be passed over lightly, and it was talked of a great deal. There were so many versions of it that it would have been an edifying thing to buy all the papers and compare them. Mr Hobbs read so much about it that he became quite bewildered. One paper described his young friend Cedric as an infant in arms—another as a young man at Oxford, winning all the honours, and distinguishing himself by writing Greek poems; one said he was engaged to a young lady of great beauty, who was the daughter of a duke; another said he had just been married; the only thing, in fact, which was *not* said was that he was a little boy between seven and eight, with handsome legs and curly hair. One said he was no relation to the Earl of Dorincourt at all, but was a small impostor who had sold newspapers and slept in the streets of New York before his mother imposed upon the family lawyer, who came to America to look for the Earl's heir. Then came the descriptions of the new Lord Fauntleroy and his mother. Sometimes she was a gipsy, sometimes an actress, sometimes a beautiful Spaniard; but it

was always agreed that the Earl of Dorincourt was her deadly
enemy, and would not acknowledge her son as his heir if he
could help it; and as there seemed to be some slight flaw in
the papers she had produced, it was expected that there would
be a long trial, which would be far more interesting than anything ever carried into court before. Mr Hobbs used to read the
papers until his head was in a whirl, and in the evening he and
Dick would talk it all over. They found out what an important
personage an Earl of Dorincourt was, and what a magnificent
income he possessed, and how many estates he owned, and
how stately and beautiful was the Castle in which he lived;
and the more they learned the more excited they became.

'Seems like somethin' orter be done,' said Mr Hobbs.
'Things like them orter be held on to—earls or no earls.'

But there really was nothing they could do but each
write a letter to Cedric, containing assurances of their friendship and sympathy. They wrote those letters as soon as they
could after receiving the news; and after having written them,
they handed them over to each other to be read.

This is what Mr Hobbs read in Dick's letter:

> DERE FREND,—i got ure letter an Mr Hobbs got his an
> we are sorry u are down on ure luck an we say hold on
> as longs u kin and dont let no one git ahed of u. There
> is a lot of ole theves wil make al they kin of u ef u
> dont kepe ure i skinned. But this is mosly to say that
> ive not forgot wot u did for me an if there aint no
> better way cum over here and go in pardners with me.
> Biznes is fine and ile see no harm cums to u. Enny big
> feler that trise to cum it over u wil hafter setle it fust
> with Perfessor Dick Tipton. So no more at present
>
> > DICK

And this was what Dick read in Mr Hobbs's letter:

> DEAR SIR,—Yrs received and wd say things looks
> bad. I believe its a put up job and them thats done it

ought to be looked after sharp. And what I write to say is two things. Im going to look this thing up. Keep quiet and I'll see a lawyer and do all I can. And if the worst happens and them earls is too many for us theres a partnership in the grocery business ready for you when yure old enough and a home and a friend in

Yrs truly,
SILAS HOBBS

'Well,' said Mr Hobbs, 'he's pervided for between us, if he ain't a earl.'

'So he is,' said Dick. 'I'd ha' stood by him. Blest if I didn't like that little feller fust rate.'

The very next morning one of Dick's customers was rather surprised. He was a young lawyer just beginning practice; as poor as a very young lawyer can possibly be, but a bright, energetic young fellow, with a sharp wit and a good temper. He had a shabby office near Dick's stand, and every morning Dick blacked his boots for him, and quite often they were not exactly watertight, but he always had a friendly word or a joke for Dick.

That particular morning, when he put his foot on the rest, he had an illustrated paper in his hand—an enterprising paper, with pictures in it of conspicuous people and things. He had just finished looking it over, and when the last boot was polished, he handed it to the boy.

'Here's a paper for you, Dick,' he said; 'you can look it over when you drop in at Delmonico's for your breakfast. Picture of an English castle in it, and an English earl's daughter-in-law. Fine young woman too — lots of hair—though she seems to be raising rather a row. You ought to become familiar with the nobility and gentry, Dick. Begin on the Right Honourable the Earl of Dorincourt and Lady Fauntleroy. Hallo! I say, what's the matter?'

The pictures he spoke of were on the front page, and

Dick was staring at one of them with his eyes and mouth open, and his sharp face almost pale with excitement.

'What's to pay, Dick?' said the young man. 'What has paralysed you?'

Dick really did look as if something tremendous had happened. He pointed to the picture, under which was written: 'Mother of Claimant (Lady Fauntleroy).'

It was the picture of a handsome woman, with large eyes and heavy braids of black hair wound around her head.

'Her!' said Dick. 'My, I know her better'n I know you!'

The young man began to laugh.

'Where did you meet her, Dick?' he said. 'At Newport? Or when you ran over to Paris the last time?'

Dick actually forgot to grin. He began to gather his brushes and things together, as if he had something to do which would put an end to his business for the present.

'Never mind,' he said. 'I know her! An' I've struck work for this morning.'

And in less than five minutes from that time he was tearing through the streets on his way to Mr Hobbs and the corner store. Mr Hobbs could scarcely believe the evidence of his senses when he looked across the counter and saw Dick rush in with the paper in his hand. The boy was out of breath with running; so much out of breath, in fact, that he could scarcely speak as he threw the paper down on the counter.

'Hallo!' exclaimed Mr Hobbs. 'Hallo! What you got there?'

'Look at it!' panted Dick. 'Look at that woman in the picture! That's what you look at! *She* ain't no 'ristocrat, *she* ain't!' with withering scorn. 'She's no lord's wife. You may eat me, if it ain't Minna—*Minna*! I'd know her anywheres, an' so'd Ben. Jest ax him.'

Mr Hobbs dropped into his seat.

'I knowed it was a put-up job,' he said. 'I knowed it; and they done it on account o' him bein' a 'Merican!'

'Done it!' cried Dick with disgust '*She* done it, that's who done it. She was allers up to her tricks; an' I'll tell yer

wot come to me, the minnit I saw her pictur'. There was one
o' them papers we saw had a letter in it that said somethin'
'bout her boy, an' it said he had a scar on his chin. Put 'em
together—he 'n' that there scar! Why that there boy o' hers
ain't no more a lord than I am! It's *Ben*'s boy—the little chap
she hit when she let fly that plate at me.'

Professor Dick Tipton had always been a sharp boy, and
earning his living in the streets of a big city had made him still
sharper. He had learned to keep his eyes open and his wits
about him, and it must be confessed he enjoyed immensely
the excitement and impatience of the moment. If little Lord
Fauntleroy could only have looked into the store that morning
he would certainly have been interested, even if all the discussion and plans had been intended to decide the fate of
some other boy than himself.

Mr Hobbs was almost overwhelmed by his sense of
responsibility, and Dick was all alive and full of energy. He
began to write a letter to Ben, and he cut out the picture and
enclosed it to him, and Mr Hobbs wrote a letter to Cedric and
one to the Earl. They were in the midst of this letter-writing
when a new idea came to Dick.

'Say,' he said, 'the feller that give me the paper, he's a
lawyer. Let's ax him what we'd better do. Lawyers knows it
all.'

Mr Hobbs was immensely impressed by this suggestion
and Dick's business capacity.

'That's so!' he replied. 'This here calls for lawyers.'

And leaving the store in care of a substitute, he struggled
into his coat and marched down town with Dick, and the two
presented themselves with their romantic story in Mr Harrison's office, much to that young man's astonishment.

If he had not been a very young lawyer, with a very
enterprising mind and a great deal of spare time on his hands,
he might not have been so readily interested in what they had
to say, for it all certainly sounded very wild and queer; but he
chanced to want something to do very much, and he chanced

to know Dick, and Dick chanced to say his say in a very sharp, telling sort of way.

'And,' said Mr Hobbs, 'say what your time's worth a' hour and look into this thing thorough, and *I*'ll pay the damage—Silas Hobbs, corner of Blank Street, Vegetables and Fancy Groceries.'

'Well,' said Mr Harrison, 'it will be a big thing if it turns out all right, and it will be almost as big a thing for me as for Lord Fauntleroy; and at any rate, no harm can be done by investigating. It appears there has been some dubiousness about the child. The woman contradicted herself in some of her statements about his age, and aroused suspicion. The first persons to be written to are Dick's brother and the Earl of Dorincourt's family lawyer.'

And actually before the sun went down, two letters had been written and sent in two different directions—one speeding out of New York harbour on a mail steamer on its way to England, and the other on a train carrying letters and passengers bound for California. And the first was addressed to 'T. Havisham Esq.', and the second to 'Benjamin Tipton'.

And after the store was closed that evening, Mr Hobbs and Dick sat in the back room and talked together until midnight.

FOURTEEN

The Exposure

It is astonishing how short a time it takes for very wonderful things to happen. It had taken only a few minutes, apparently, to change all the fortunes of the little boy dangling his red legs from the high stool in Mr Hobbs's store, and to transform him from a small boy, living the simplest life in a quiet street, into an English nobleman, the heir to an earldom and magnificent wealth. It had taken only a few minutes, apparently, to change him from an English nobleman into a penniless little impostor, with no right to any of the splendours he had been enjoying. And surprising as it may appear, it did not take nearly so long a time as one might have expected to alter the face of everything again and to give back to him all that he had been in danger of losing.

It took the less time because, after all, the woman who had called herself Lady Fauntleroy was not nearly so clever as she was wicked; and when she had been closely pressed by Mr Havisham's questions about her marriage and her boy, she had made one or two blunders which had caused suspicion to be awakened; and then she had lost her presence of mind and her temper, and in her excitement and anger had betrayed herself still further. All the mistakes she made were about her child. There seemed no doubt that she had been

161

married to Bevis, Lord Fauntleroy, and had quarrelled with him and had been paid to keep away from him; but Mr Havisham found out that her story of the boy's being born in a certain part of London was false; and just when they all were in the midst of the commotion caused by this discovery, there came the letter from the young lawyer in New York, and Mr Hobbs's letters also.

What an evening it was when those letters arrived, and when Mr Havisham and the Earl sat and talked their plans over in the library!

'After my first three meetings with her,' said Mr Havisham, 'I began to suspect her strongly. It appeared to me that the child was older than she said he was, and she made a slip in speaking of the date of his birth and then tried to patch the matter up. The story these letters bring fits in with several of my suspicions. Our best plan will be to cable at once for these two Tiptons, say nothing about them to her, and suddenly confront her with them when she is not expecting it. She is only a very clumsy plotter after all. My opinion is that she will be frightened out of her wits, and will betray herself on the spot.'

And that was what actually happened. She was told nothing, and Mr Havisham kept her from suspecting anything by continuing to have interviews with her, in which he assured her he was investigating her statements; and she really began to feel so secure that her spirits rose immensely and she began to be as insolent as might have been expected.

But one fine morning, as she sat in her sitting-room at the inn called the Dorincourt Arms, making some very fine plans for herself, Mr Havisham was announced; and when he entered he was followed by no less than three persons—one was a sharp-faced boy and one was a big young man, and the third was the Earl of Dorincourt.

She sprang to her feet and actually uttered a cry of terror. It broke from her before she had time to check it. She had thought of these newcomers as being thousands of miles away, when she had ever thought of them at all, which she had scarcely done for years. She had never expected to see them again. It must be confessed that Dick grinned a little when he saw her.

'Hallo, Minna!' he said.

The big young man—who was Ben—stood still a minute and looked at her.

'Do you know her?' Mr Havisham asked, glancing from one to the other.

'Yes,' said Ben. 'I know her and she knows me.' And he turned his back on her and went and stood looking out of the window as if the sight of her was hateful to him, as indeed it was. Then the woman, seeing herself so baffled and exposed, lost all control over herself and flew into such a rage as Ben and Dick had often seen her in before. Dick grinned a trifle more as he watched her and heard the names she called them all and the violent threats she made, but Ben did not turn to look at her.

'I can swear to her in any court,' he said to Mr Havisham, 'and I can bring a dozen others who will. Her father is a respectable sort of man, though he's low down in the world. Her mother was just like herself. She's dead, but he's alive, and he's honest enough to be ashamed of her. He'll tell you who she is, and whether she married me or not.'

Then he clenched his hand suddenly and turned on her.

'Where's the child?' he demanded. 'He's going with me! He is done with you and so am I!'

And just as he finished saying the words, the door leading into the bedroom opened a little, and the boy, probably attracted by the sound of the loud voices, looked in. He was not a handsome boy, but he had rather a nice face, and he was quite like Ben, his father, as anyone could see, and there was the three-cornered scar on his chin.

Ben walked up to him and took his hand, and his own was trembling.

'Yes,' he said, 'I could swear to him too. Tom,' he said to the little fellow, 'I'm your father, I've come to take you away. Where's your hat?'

The boy pointed to where it lay on a chair. It evidently rather pleased him to hear he was going away. He had been so accustomed to queer experiences that it did not surprise him to be told by a stranger that he was his father. He objected so much to the woman who had come a few months before to the place where he had lived since his babyhood, and who had suddenly announced that she was his mother, that he was quite ready for a change. Ben took up the hat and marched to the door.

'If you want me again,' he said to Mr Havisham, 'you know where to find me.'

He walked out of the room, holding the child's hand and not looking at the woman once. She was fairly raving with fury, and the Earl was calmly gazing at her through his eye-glasses, which he had quietly placed upon his aristocratic eagle nose.

'Come, come, my young woman,' said Mr Havisham. 'This won't do at all. If you don't want to be locked up, you really must behave yourself.'

And there was something so very business-like in his tones that, probably feeling that the safest thing she could do would be to get out of the way, she gave him one savage look and dashed past him into the next room and slammed the door.

'We shall have no more trouble with her,' said Mr Havisham.

And he was right; for that very night she left the Dorincourt Arms and took the train to London, and was seen no more.

When the Earl left the room after the interview he went at once to his carriage.

'To Court Lodge,' he said to Thomas.

'To Court Lodge,' said Thomas to the coachman as he mounted the box, 'an' you may depend on it, things is taking a uniggspected turn.'

When the carriage stopped at Court Lodge, Cedric was in the drawing-room with his mother.

The Earl came in without being announced. He looked an inch or so taller and a great many years younger. His deep eyes flashed.

'Where,' he said, 'is Lord Fauntleroy?'

Mrs Errol came forward, a flush rising to her cheek. 'Is it Lord Fauntleroy?' she asked. 'Is it indeed?' The Earl put out his hand and grasped hers.

'Yes,' he answered, 'it is.'

Then he put his other hand on Cedric's shoulder.

'Fauntleroy,' he said in his unceremonious, authoritative way, 'ask your mother when she will come to us at the Castle.'

Fauntleroy flung his arms around his mother's neck.

'To live with us!' he cried. 'To live with us always!'

The Earl looked at Mrs Errol, and Mrs Errol looked at the Earl. His lordship was entirely in earnest. He had made up his mind to waste no time in arranging this matter. He had begun to think it would suit him to make friends with his heir's mother.

'Are you quite sure you want me?' said Mrs Errol with her soft, pretty smile.

'Quite sure,' he said bluntly. 'We have always wanted you, but we were not exactly aware of it. We hope you will come.'

FIFTEEN

His Eighth Birthday

Ben took his boy and went back to his cattle ranch in California, and he returned under very comfortable circumstances. Just before his going Mr Havisham had an interview with him in which the lawyer told him that the Earl of Dorincourt wished to do something for the boy who might have turned out to be Lord Fauntleroy, and so he had decided that it would be a good plan to invest in a cattle ranch of his own, and put Ben in charge of it on terms which would make it pay him very well, and which would lay a foundation for his son's future. And so when Ben went away he went as the prospective master of a ranch which would be almost as good as his own, and might easily become his own in time, as indeed it did in the course of a few years; and Tom, the boy, grew up on it into a fine young man and was devotedly fond of his father; and they were so successful and happy that Ben used to say that Tom made up to him for all the troubles he had ever had.

But Dick and Mr Hobbs—who had actually come over with the others to see that things were properly looked after—did not return for some time. It had been decided at the outset that the Earl would provide for Dick, and would see that he received a solid education; and Mr Hobbs had decided that as he himself had left a reliable substitute in charge of his store, he could afford to wait to see the festivities which were to celebrate Lord Fauntleroy's eighth birthday. All the tenantry were invited, and there were to be feasting and dancing and games in the park, and bonfires and fireworks in the evening.

'Just like the Fourth of July!' said Lord Fauntleroy. 'It seems a pity my birthday wasn't on the Fourth, doesn't it? For then we could keep them both together.'

It must be confessed that at first the Earl and Mr Hobbs were not as intimate as it might have been hoped they would become, in the interests of the British Aristocracy. The fact was that the Earl had known very few grocery-men and Mr Hobbs had not had many close acquaintances who were earls; and so in their rare interviews conversation did not flourish. It must also be owned that Mr Hobbs had been rather over-whelmed by the splendours Fauntleroy felt it his duty to show him.

The entrance gate and the stone lions and the avenue impressed Mr Hobbs somewhat at the beginning, and when he saw the Castle and the flower gardens and the hothouses and the terraces and the peacocks and the dungeon and the armour and the great staircase and the stables and the liveried servants, he really was quite bewildered. But it was the picture gallery which seemed to be the finishing stroke.

'Somethin' in the manner of a museum?' he said to Fauntleroy, when he was led into the great beautiful room.

'N-no—!' said Fauntleroy rather doubtfully. 'I don't *think* it's a museum. My grandfather says these are my ancestors.'

'Your aunt's sisters!' ejaculated Mr Hobbs. '*All* of 'em. Your great-uncle, he *must* have had a family! Did he raise 'em all?'

And he sank into a seat and looked around him with an agitated countenance, until with the greatest difficulty Lord Fauntleroy managed to explain that the walls were not lined entirely with the portraits of the progeny of his great-uncle.

He found it necessary, in fact, to call in the assistance of

Mrs Mellon, who knew all about the pictures, and could tell who painted them and when, and who added romantic stories of the lords and ladies who were the originals. When Mr Hobbs once understood, and had heard some of these stories, he was very much fascinated and liked the picture gallery almost better than anything else; and he would often walk over from the village where he stayed at the Dorincourt Arms, and would spend half an hour or so wandering about the gallery, staring at the painted ladies and gentlemen who also stared at him, and shaking his head nearly all the time.

'And they was all earls,' he would say, 'or pretty nigh it! An' *he*'s goin' to be one of 'em, an' own it all!'

Privately he was not nearly so much disgusted with earls and their mode of life as he had expected to be, and it is to be doubted whether his strictly Republican principles were not shaken a little by a closer acquaintance with castles and ancestors and all the rest of it. At any rate, one day he uttered a very remarkable and unexpected sentiment.

'I wouldn't have minded bein' one of 'em myself!' he said—which was really a great concession.

What a grand day it was when little Lord Fauntleroy's birthday arrived, and how his young lordship enjoyed it! How beautiful the park looked, filled with the thronging people dressed in their gayest and best, and with the flags flying from the tents and the top of the Castle! Nobody had stayed away who could possibly come, because everybody was really glad that little Lord Fauntleroy was to be little Lord Fauntleroy still, and some day was to be the master of everything. Everyone wanted to have a look at him, and at his pretty, kind mother, who had made so many friends. And positively everyone liked the Earl rather better, and felt more amiably towards him because the little boy loved and trusted him so, and because, also, he had now made friends with and behaved respectfully to his heir's mother. It was said that he was even beginning to be fond of her too, and that between his young lordship and his young lordship's mother, the Earl might be changed in time into quite a well-behaved old nobleman, and everybody might be happier and better off.

What scores and scores of people there were under the trees, and in the tents, and on the lawns! Farmers and farmers' wives in their Sunday suits and bonnets and shawls; girls and their sweethearts; children frolicking and chasing about; and old dames in red cloaks gossiping together. At the Castle there were ladies and gentlemen who had come to see the fun, and to congratulate the Earl, and to meet Mrs Errol. Lady Lorridaile and Sir Harry were there, and Sir Thomas Asshe and his daughters, and Mr Havisham of course; and then beautiful Miss Vivian Herbert, with the loveliest white gown and lace parasol, and a circle of gentlemen to take care of her—though she evidently liked Fauntleroy better than all of them put together. And when he saw her and ran to her and put his arms around her neck, she put her arms around him too, and kissed him as warmly as if he had been her own favourite little brother, and she said:

'Dear little Lord Fauntleroy! Dear little boy! I am so glad! I am so glad!'

And afterwards she walked about the grounds with him, and let him show her everything. And when he took her to where Mr Hobbs and Dick were, and said to her, 'This is my old, old friend Mr Hobbs, Miss Herbert, and this is my other old friend Dick. I told them how pretty you were, and I told them they should see you if you came to my birthday'—she shook hands with them both, and stood and talked to them in her prettiest way, asking them about America and their voyage and their life since they had been in England; while Fauntleroy stood by, looking up at her with adoring eyes, and his cheeks quite flushed with delight because he saw that Mr Hobbs and Dick liked her so much.

'Well,' said Dick solemnly afterwards, 'she's the daisiest gal I ever saw! She's—well, she's just daisy, that's what she is, 'n' no mistake!'

Everybody looked after her as she passed, and everyone looked after little Lord Fauntleroy. And the sun shone and the flags fluttered and the games were played and the dances danced, and as the gaieties went on and the joyous afternoon passed, his little lordship was simply radiantly happy.

The whole world seemed beautiful to him.

There was someone else who was happy too—an old man, who, though he had been rich and noble all his life, had not often been very honestly happy. Perhaps indeed I shall tell you that I think it was because he was rather better than he had been that he was rather happier. He had not indeed suddenly become as good as Fauntleroy thought him; but at least he had begun to love something, and he had several times found a sort of pleasure in doing the kind things which the innocent, kind little heart of a child had suggested—and that was a beginning. And every day he had been more pleased with his son's wife. It was true, as the people said, that he was beginning to like her too. He liked to hear her sweet voice and to see her sweet face; and as he sat in his armchair, he used to watch her and listen as she talked to her boy; and he heard loving, gentle words which were new to him, and he began to see why the little fellow who had lived in a New York side street, and known grocery-men and made friends with boot-blacks, was still so well bred and manly a little fellow that he made no one ashamed of him, even when fortune changed him into the heir to an English earldom, living in an English castle.

It was really a very simple thing after all—it was only that he had lived near a kind and gentle heart, and had been taught to think kind thoughts always and to care for others. It is a very little thing, perhaps, but it is the best thing of all. He knew nothing of earls and castles; he was quite ignorant of all grand and splendid things; but he was always lovable because he was simple and loving. To be so is like being born a king.

As the old Earl of Dorincourt looked at him that day, moving about the park among the people, talking to those he knew and making his ready little bow when anyone greeted him, entertaining his friends Dick and Mr Hobbs, or standing near his mother or Miss Herbert listening to their conversation, the old nobleman was very well satisfied with him. And he had never been better satisfied than he was when they went down to the biggest tent, where the more important tenants of the Dorincourt estate were sitting down to the grand collation of the day.

They were drinking toasts; and, after they had drunk the health of the Earl with much more enthusiasm than his name had ever been greeted with before, they proposed the health of 'Little Lord Fauntleroy'. And if there had ever been any doubt at all as to whether his lordship was popular or not, it would have been settled that instant. Such a clamour of voices and such a rattle of glasses and applause! They had begun to like him so much, those warm-hearted people, that they forgot to feel any restraint before the ladies and gentlemen from the Castle, who had come to see them. They made quite a decent uproar, and one or two motherly women looked tenderly at the little fellow where he stood, with his mother on one side and the Earl on the other, and grew quite moist about the eyes, and said to one another:

'God bless him, the pretty little dear!'

Little Lord Fauntleroy was delighted. He stood and smiled, and made bows, and flushed rosy red with pleasure up to the roots of his bright hair.

'Is it because they like me, Dearest?' he said to his mother. 'Is it, Dearest? I'm so glad!'

And then the Earl put his hand on the child's shoulder and said to him:

'Fauntleroy, say to them that you thank them for their kindness.'

Fauntleroy gave a glance up at him and then at his mother.

'Must I?' he asked just a trifle shyly, and she smiled, and so did Miss Herbert, and they both nodded. And so he made a little step forward, and everybody looked at him— such a beautiful, innocent little fellow he was, too, with his brave, trustful face!—and he spoke as loudly as he could, his childish voice ringing out quite clear and strong.

'I'm ever so much obliged to you!' he said, 'and—I hope you'll enjoy my birthday—because I've enjoyed it so much—and—I'm very glad I'm going to be an earl—I didn't think at first I should like it, but now I do—and I love this place so, and I think it is beautiful—and—and—and when I am an earl, I am going to try to be as good as my grandfather.'

And amid the shouts and clamour of applause, he stepped back with a little sigh of relief, and put his hand into the Earl's and stood close to him, smiling and leaning against his side.

And that would be the very end of my story; but I must add one curious piece of information, which is that Mr Hobbs became so fascinated with high life and was so reluctant to leave his young friend that he actually sold his corner store in New York, and settled in the English village of Erlesboro, where he opened a shop which was patronized by the Castle and consequently was a great success. And though he and the Earl never became very intimate, if you will believe me, that man Hobbs became in time more aristocratic than his lordship himself, and he read the Court news every morning, and followed all the doings of the House of Lords! And about ten years after, when Dick who had finished his education and was going to visit his brother in California, asked the good grocer if he did not wish to return to America, he shook his head seriously.

'Not to live there,' he said. 'Not to live there; I want to be near *him*, an' sort o' look after him. It's a good enough country for them that's young an' stirrin'—but there's faults in it. There's not an aunt-sister among 'em—nor a earl!'

Bantam Classics bring you the world's greatest literature—books that have stood the test of time—at specially low prices. These beautifully designed books will be proud additions to your bookshelf. You'll want all these time-tested classics for your own reading pleasure.

Titles by Thomas Hardy:

☐	21191	JUDE THE OBSCURE	$2.95
☐	21024	THE MAYOR OF CASTERBRIDGE	$1.95
☐	21080	THE RETURN OF THE NATIVE	$2.95
☐	21168	TESS OF THE D'UBERVILLES	$2.95
☐	21257	FAR FROM THE MADDING CROWD	$2.95

Titles by the Brontës:

☐	21140	JANE EYRE Charlotte Brontë	$1.95
☐	21258	WUTHERING HEIGHTS Emily Brontë	$2.25

Titles by Jane Austen:

☐	21159	EMMA	$1.95
☐	21121	MANSFIELD PARK	$3.50
☐	21137	PERSUASION	$2.95
☐	21215	PRIDE AND PREJUDICE	$1.95
☐	21110	SENSE AND SENSIBILITY	$2.50
☐	21197	NORTHANGER ABBEY	$2.50

Buy them at your local bookstore or use this handy coupon for ordering:

Bantam Classics bring you the world's greatest literature—books that have stood the test of time—at specially low prices. These beautifully designed books will be proud additions to your bookshelf. You'll want all these time-tested classics for your own reading pleasure.

☐ 21105	ROBINSON CRUSOE, Daniel Defoe	$1.95
☐ 21232	GULLIVER'S TRAVELS & OTHER WRITINGS, Jonathan Swift	$2.95
☐ 21032	THE HUNCHBACK OF NOTRE DAME, Victor Hugo	$1.95
☐ 21247	FRANKENSTEIN, Mary Shelley	$1.95
☐ 21148	DRACULA, Bram Stoker	$1.95

Titles by Robert Louis Stevenson:

☐ 21200	DR. JEKYLL AND MR. HYDE	$2.50
☐ 21260	KIDNAPPED	$1.95
☐ 21249	TREASURE ISLAND	$1.95

Titles by Alexander Dumas:

☐ 21187	THE COUNT OF MONTE CRISTO	$3.50
☐ 21217	THE THREE MUSKETEERS	$4.50

Titles by H. G. Wells:

☐ 21253	THE INVISIBLE MAN	$2.50
☐ 21239	THE TIME MACHINE	$2.50

Titles by Rudyard Kipling:

☐ 21190	CAPTAINS COURAGEOUS	$1.95
☐ 21117	KIM	$2.25
☐ 21199	THE JUNGLE BOOK & JUST SO STORIES	$3.95

Titles by Jules Verne:

☐ 21145	AROUND THE WORLD IN EIGHTY DAYS	$2.25
☐ 21252	20,000 LEAGUES UNDER THE SEA	$2.50